HEIGHTENED LOVE

HEIGHTENED LOVE

ALIZA ALI JANNAT

BLUEROSE PUBLISHERS
India | U.K.

Copyright © Aliza Ali Jannat 2024

All rights reserved by author. No part of this publication may be reproduced, stored in a retrieval system or transmitted in any form or by any means, electronic, mechanical, photocopying, recording or otherwise, without the prior permission of the author. Although every precaution has been taken to verify the accuracy of the information contained herein, the publisher assumes no responsibility for any errors or omissions. No liability is assumed for damages that may result from the use of information contained within.

BlueRose Publishers takes no responsibility for any damages, losses, or liabilities that may arise from the use or misuse of the information, products, or services provided in this publication.

For permissions requests or inquiries regarding this publication, please contact:

BLUEROSE PUBLISHERS
www.BlueRoseONE.com
info@bluerosepublishers.com
+91 8882 898 898
+4407342408967

ISBN: 978-93-6783-853-2

Cover Design: Sadhna Kumari
Typesetting: Pooja Sharma

First Edition: December 2024

To my parents, whose unwavering support has meant the world to me, and to my siblings, whose love has always been a treasured gift. This one's for you.

"Honour your past, but do not be too afraid to carve a new path towards your future."

— *Aliza Ali Jannat*

DISCLAIMER

This book is a work of fiction, born entirely from the author's imagination. Any names, characters, events, or settings that may seem familiar are purely coincidental and should not be interpreted as representations of real people, places, or occurrences. The author has exercised creative liberty to craft this story, and it is intended to be read and understood as a fictional narrative. Any resemblance to actual events or individuals is unintended and incidental.

CONTENTS

PREFACE	1
STRANGERS IN THE NIGHT	5
THE DREAM GIRL	26
WHEN I SEE YOU AGAIN	38
THE BEAUTIFUL GAME OF DESTINY	51
TOGETHER IS MY FAVOURITE PLACE TO BE	69
YOU IN EVERY BREATH	84
AND THE DANCING IN THE RAIN	104
DO I REALLY KNOW YOU AFTER ALL?	121
THE WHITE LIES	137
I LOVE YOU!	153
THE WALK OF THORNS	165
THE JADED LOVER	177
THE BRAVE HEART	190
EPILOGUE	204
ACKNOWLEDGMENTS	206
AUTHOR'S NOTE	210

PREFACE

For as long as I can remember, I have been drawn to the raw, unfiltered realities of human lives and emotions. Each of us carries silent battles within, navigating them with resilience while often presenting a brave smile to the world. Interestingly, even the strongest among us experience sleepless nights, moments of doubt, and a vulnerability we rarely acknowledge. Society conditions us to suppress our emotions, pain, and struggles, urging us to conform to norms. Yet, I believe we are the unsung heroes of our lives—offering love, support, and encouragement to others while seldom applauding ourselves for the courage it takes to simply keep going. How fascinating it is that while we are so similar in essence, we remain unique in the way we live, feel, and love.

This book, though a work of fiction, was born from innumerable moments of reflection and a desire to make sense of the complexities that shape our existence. My intention was not only to tell a story but to explore the intricacies of human emotions in a way that feels real and relatable. Great care has been taken to capture the nuances of anxiety, family dysfunction, physical and mental abuse, and other difficult realities, as they are experiences shared by many. While the characters and their journeys are imagined, the emotions they feel are grounded in truth. I wanted readers to see themselves in these pages, to feel connected, and to immerse themselves in a story that resonates on a deeply personal level.

At its core, this book is a story of reflection—one that bridges the universal appeal of first love with the profound lessons of a love that evolves and deepens over time. It explores imperfections, revealing the raw beauty and strength found in vulnerability. In an age that celebrates perfection, this story serves as a reminder that authenticity, in all its messiness, is what makes us human.

The journey of crafting this book has been one of immense self-discovery. Though fictional, the story required me to dig deeply into the emotional weight of its themes, ensuring every word felt genuine and impactful. There were sleepless nights and many moments of exhaustion as I worked to balance this project with my career and personal life. Yet, halfway through, I realised this book was more than just a story; it was a mirror, reflecting the shared struggles and triumphs of many lives. That realisation gave me the determination to keep going, knowing how important it was to honour these emotions truthfully.

Through this book, I hope readers find solace, strength, and a deeper understanding of their own lives. It is my belief that this story will inspire you to embrace your own journey with courage and compassion. Life, after all, is a little tilted and a little bumpy–but that's what makes it uniquely yours. May this book encourage you to cherish your highs and find meaning in your lows, as both are integral to the beauty of your story.

Thank you for choosing to embark on this journey with me. It is an honour to share this piece of my heart with you, and I hope this book becomes a companion, a guide, or simply a comforting voice on your path.

STRANGERS IN THE NIGHT

...Know that you are the painter of your life, you decide the colours, the themes, the patterns and when you finish the painting, have a firm faith and believe that you have created a masterpiece, irrespective of the spectators or the people around you who may or may not believe the same...You need to have faith in the work, the effort, the creativity, and the love you poured into creating this masterpiece: YOUR LIFE! Cherish it...

"We have been looking for you everywhere and look at you, as usual gazing and gawking at the moon. I just don't get it. What is it with you and the moon, Zunaisa? I hope one day you don't come out and identify yourself as a werewolf," chuckled Shanaya.

Zunaisa was extremely fond of Shanaya and adored her not because she was her sister but also because she was her confidant, her first friend she ever made, and she practically shared all her life with her; just like any other sibling in the world they both had their days of war and the days of absolute symphony oscillating from time to time. Zunaisa admired Shanaya's boldness and the bodacious girl that she was, she was happy to have found a friend in her sister.

"Now come on, you, or are you still going to be here and looking at the moon all night?? Come on! Let's go, we are organising a bonfire and some fun games," Shanaya winked at her.

By now, Zunaisa who was quiet all along, broke her silence and pulled Shanaya across the other end of the open garden, which had beautiful and large wooden benches that complemented the lush green garden filled with flowers of different kinds, shapes, and colours; some of them seemed like local herbal plants, but all of it together created a refreshing spot to soak and breathe in. It was a fairly lit night; one could even spot Jupiter with their naked eye, and there were a number of constellations occupying the sky; the full moon added just the right amount of allure to the night. The moon rather appeared brighter, bigger and well illuminated, the cold breeze, the soothing fragrance of the flowers, the rustic benches-all of it felt straight out of someone's vision of poetry.

"Sssh!" Zunaisa hushed Shanaya who was all prepared to speak. "Just sit here and look above, do you see how beautiful the moon is? It is the 14th of the lunar calendar which means it's a full moon. Look around, one can see everything around just with this moonlight, and unfortunately even your face is visible too, haha!" Zunaisa burst into fits of laughter. Shanaya rolled her eyes at her, and she almost got up to leave but Zunaisa held her hand and gently nudged her and said, "You know I love you, right? I mean ugh, but yes, I do. I can't live with you and cannot live without you," she hugged her lovingly. This was yet another healthy banter between the sisters, and Shanaya took it sportingly.

"Hello ladies! I hope I am not interrupting a full-blown girls' session, and if anything, could you scoot a bit, Zunaisa? I would love to be the third wheel here and listen to your gross rants and even pitch in if I may," Rey smirked and chuckled.

"Oh, please Rey! Do not act like you are interrupting, you are joining us on an all-girls' trip. That too at my bachelorette party says that you are the third wheel here anyway." Shanaya lashed at him. "Wow, wow! Calm down bride to be, what would your fiancé think if he saw you all raged up like this? Save the tantrums for my brother-in-law." He laughed it off. Shanaya gave Rey a death glare and almost prepared some pinpointing words to hurl back at him and that is when Zunaisa intervened. "Please, you guys! Can you both stop this unnecessary jibe already? I mean, we are here to enjoy and spend time with each other. Let us not get into silly arguments and spoil our night and the trip. Now come on, let us join others back at the bonfire and cherish the night and just before we leave, can you both please for a moment have a quick look at what I wrote today? I am really hoping I can add this to my blog for my readers." She gave her siblings, Shanaya and Rey, her irresistible, innocent-looking, charming stare, and lo behold, nobody could ever evade her cherubic doe eyes, not even her siblings.

Zunaisa had a certain something about her, she had exquisitely sharp features, her hair when she would let loose would flow effortlessly below her waist; the colour of her hair was deep chestnut brown hair, her eyebrows were naturally arched; and her lips were full and plump with a cupid's bow, adding more charm and sensuality to her already blessed looks. But apart from her graceful looks there was something likeable about her which always made her stand apart from the crowd, her demeanour, her aura was very positive and magnetic; whenever she would be around people, everyone couldn't help but notice her and be drawn to her. She carried herself with great poise; she was a grounded person and well rooted. Zunaisa was passionate about helping others and always tried her best to give love and respect to everyone she met irrespective of their stature; her motto in life was to "GIVE LOVE AND GET LOVE," quite quaint to the popular modern belief. Some of her friends and acquaintances did take a dig at her at times and thought that she was being naïve, but Zunaisa was determined that she would create a legacy of her own, filled with love, kindness and empathy. She wasn't one of those who would succumb to the popular belief system;

she believed in charting unknown paths, embracing the uncertainty. Isn't uncertainty in life the only certainty in life? Zunaisa surely did believe so.

"Alright, alright! Stop it with your doe eyes now and show us what you have written," Rey retorted. Zunaisa smiled and jumped out of her seat with all the excitement to show her writing to her confidants. She would maintain a vivid diary for her writings and penning her thoughts. The one that she had, had a vintage touch to it, the cover of the diary had a leather-like texture and a dangling bookmark to it which had her initials engraved; the paper of the diary were off white in shade and had a coarse texture, it was one of the biggest treasures she possessed and cherished the most. She flipped through the coarse pages, which made a rhythmic sound as the pages were being turned over; to show what she had written for her next blog.

It read: *"And just like the moon, we all go through phases, we wax and wane in our periodic rhythm which is unique to our own. And thus, just like the moon, we too have flaws, we have our days of darkness and some pitfalls. However, after completing our cycle of darkness, we come back up, shining bigger, brighter and more beautiful with all the light and experience we gathered during those moments. We must remember, we all go through phases, we wax and wane at our pace, and our experiences reform us, making us truly special and unique in our own true sense."*

"Wow! Zee, this is one piece of work. Proud of you." Shanaya's eyes were twinkling with joy and were filled with immense pride for Zunaisa's naturally gifted skills of articulation and eloquence. Rey, on the other hand, although wasn't an ardent lover of poetry and prose, but he was the type of a brother who would actually even end up reading a book if it would make her sisters happy. He was equally happy and proud of her. "You still have the time; you might as well become a full-time author and ditch this lawyer thing of yours. You surely are a damn good writer, Sis!" said Rey.

Zunaisa was overjoyed to know her siblings loved her writing; she took their opinion really seriously. "Thank you, guys, I was close to sure that I wrote something awesome but needed a push, so thanks for that. And about being an author instead of a lawyer, I think you have lost your mind, Rey; I write because it makes me happy and I do not wish to pursue it professionally. I think some pursuits in life should be left as it is and should be enjoyed without the baggage of fear or constant need for success, they should just be an outlet for us to feel alive and happy." Just then their tête-à-tête was interrupted by Prakriti. "Hello, gorgeous people! Sorry, to intervene in this very philosophical session which I couldn't help but overhear from afar but I hope that you do realise we all have been waiting for you all to start our bonfire and games, right? Now, let's go, before it gets too late. But, on second thoughts, the darker the night, the better it is for us, and be as it may few games are best enjoyed in the darkness of night." Prakriti jokingly winked at them, she was one of the most adventurous and spontaneous amongst them, she was always ready for any situation irrespective of the unambiguity or impending danger that might follow, she remained unfazed at the face of it. She was known for her solo trips, rides and dates and what not. She was truly a carefree soul who lived life on her own terms and pushed herself to do something different and daring each day.

Thereafter, all of them marched back towards their property, whistling, singing, and chatting all along. The youthful years of life are something to be cherished about: one is carefree but also not entirely careless. As a young adult, life seems to have its own ups and down, you want to live the present to the fullest and not care about tomorrow, but at times, you are hit by the reality of life, and then you get consumed by the feelings of crippling anxieties; feeling hopeless and desperate to salvage the plight life throws at you. Yet, in moments like these, surrounded by friends, you forget it all, if only for a while.

Soon they retreated, and then they all joined others at the bonfire. The group was sitting warm and cosily, circling around the bonfire. Shanaya's close friends from school and college: Ritu, Akanksha, Shreya, and Urvi were already there waiting for these four to join them. "There you are, Madam Bride to be! Where have you guys been? We have been waiting for you since ages! The night is young waiting to be unravelled," Ritu giggled.

"Now without further ado, shall we jump into the game, ladies?" added Rey. Then they all sat together, passing on food and drinks. The table spread set across had some sumptuous, aromatic Pan-Asian cuisine, the drinks were pretty colourful and funky, with a twist of flavourful concoctions. The tiny outing was covered with warm lights hanging from the tree and some wired warm lights dangling across the fences of the area they were sitting in. The cool breeze and full moon nightadded more to the enchanting space.

"The rules are simple, nobody, I repeat, nobody can say NO, to anything, whether it is a task or a question, you have to do what you are told, no evading things." Prakriti voiced out the rules with utmost enthusiasm. "Oh God! Prakriti, you can make the simplest of things sound super scandalous even when they aren't," Ritu started laughing and everybody too, burst into fits of laughter; as they all unanimously agreed that Prakriti was always on the edge, ready to jump in and turn things mischievous. So, they all began their rendezvous, singing, chatting, and playing along enjoying their party. All of them then turned to raise a toast and give a short speech for the bride to be who was all set to venture on a new journey in her life.

They were reminiscing about the good times they shared and what all awaits now that the wedding was around the corner, they all spoke their hearts out. They were discussing the decorations, the venue, the bridesmaid and best man duties, and so much more. Akanksha was the quietest in their group, although she had broken up years ago, she somehow wasn't able to move on from the guy she was engaged to marry, and one could only imagine how tough it might be for her; but this is how life is.

One has to accept what it throws at you; whether you take it sportingly or you sit for days trying to resist the inevitable; changes are inevitable and the sooner a person understands that the better it is for them. It does not necessarily extinguish the pain and agony, but somehow the acceptance of the challenge becomes a tool to fight the odds and face it head on.

Acceptance of hard turns and twists in life isn't a promising or a sweet feeling, however it eventually helps to sail through our boats despite the turbulence. Akanksha finally decided to break her silence. Her eyes got numb as she couldn't help but recall her ex and the times she had spent with him. "I miss him and no matter what I do, everything around me seems to remind me of him, I wonder if he misses me too," Akanksha started sobbing. Shanaya, Ritu, and Urvi hugged her tight in order to pacify her and bring her at ease.

To subdue the sudden air of remorse, Prakriti intervened, "I don't intend to pry here but I guess we must resume our game, the bottle has given its verdict, and it is Zunaisa's turn now, she will pick her choice whether she wants to do a dare or tell us a truth; although I really do hope she will spice up the night by picking up a dare since most of you have kept it super safe up until now. My champ Zee what is it going to be? TRUTH OR DARE?" Prakriti seemingly left no stone unturned in pushing Zunaisa to select nothing but dare as her option and so she did. Prakriti overjoyed decided voluntarily that she would decide what the dare for Zunaisa would be.

"Zee, I want you to take a look around or maybe walk around and the next guy that you find, I want you to go speak to him and exchange numbers with him." Urvi protested, "You are being silly Prakriti, why would ask her to do something like that, we cannot be sure of the intentions, we are pretty away from the city in a secluded property, if things go south how on Earth would anybody help us, the hotel staff have almost retreated to their quarters. I think it is a terrible idea." Prakriti rolled her eyes at Urvi and told her that she was being a spoilt sport here and asked her to tone it down a bit and allow Zunaisa to proceed with her dare.

Zunaisa, on the other hand, even though did feel a bit jittery about the dare was determined that she would face the challenge by mustering all the courage that she has and pushing herself outside her comfort zone. She tried to diffuse the tension between Prakriti and Urvi with some of her sweet chuckles, as the odds of bumping into someone at that hour rather seemed impossible, and in her head, she was convinced that this dare wasn't as spooky as it sounded so she decided to proceed with it.

As explained, she had to take a walk around the property, and whoever she finds next, she had to speak to that person and, as suggested exchange numbers as well. Zunaisa got up and started strolling around the property, she slowly moved past the bonfire and then headed towards the corridors of the property which had an old-world charm to them. The pillars had what it occurred to be: immaculate Persian calligraphy engraved on them and from afar it added further depth, character, and opulence to the property. The tiles were interestingly designed and had a fitting combination of black and white blocks. As she walked past the floor, her tan brown stilettos made a distinctive sound of their own. The entire property was owned by an old couple who had constructed it with a vision to turn it into a place where one could unwind and break the monotony of life far away from the hustling, bustling culture of the big cities. The space sure did have a flair of its own, the property was built on a large plot, which was spread across acres. It also had a few tiny private quarters for the staff members, a pantry, a stable and storage for the livestock, and much more. They were all painted white, as if to preserve a sense of synchronicity, and a grand theme was constructed around it.

While she was still casually strolling through the corridors and walking past it, she spotted the same open garden and the wooden benches where she was sitting earlier, only to find a figure sitting there quietly. At first, Zunaisa got alarmed, thinking she was just hallucinating things as it was already close to 2 am and it did not seem practical for anybody to be up this late. Most of the guests had registered for an early morning hike across the mountain and hence there wasn't room for speculation that any guest could be out at this hour or even any staff member for that matter. She gasped at the sight and had goosebumps. She had heard from some of the staff members who were mentioning that mountains and other secluded areas often invite spirits, and such paranormal activities tend to happen there all the time.

All of these thoughts started to play and hog on her mind relentlessly, she shut her eyes and placed her hands on her ears as though she just wanted to hush and shun those whispers and creeping thoughts; she shook her head in denial. She then took a deep breath to calm herself down and decided to get closer to the benches to confirm if it was just a hallucination or if there was really something or someone sitting there. What was supposed to be a simple and fun trip; was somehow turning out to be eerie and uncanny for her. She gathered herself, there wasn't enough lighting in the garden except a faint light coming from distant lamp across the pavement of the property that connected the garden but the moonlight made things rather visible than usual.

As she got closer and closer, her heart was racing and throbbing, the feeling of the unknown ignited feelings of anxiety and nervousness. She was fidgeting her fingers in anticipation and walked further close to the shadow. To her surprise, her inhibitions of anything paranormal soon subsided when she finally reached the benches.

She could see that there was a well-built man sitting with his legs crossed, all tucked up in a white sweatshirt, joggers, and white sneakers, a deep musk fragrance lingering around him that seamlessly blended into an irresistible fragrance, all around complementing and fusing well with the soft floral scents emanating from the flowers in the garden. He was casually flicking through his cell phone engrossed in a world of his own. She was relieved at the sight that it wasn't a ghost after all, she took a deep sigh of relief.

Just then the man turned around and was startled to find Zunaisa nervously standing behind him. One could easily make out that the man appeared rather a tad bit perplexed and surprised to find a girl out in the open at such an odd hour. For several seconds he kept looking at her, thinking and contemplating if he should step up and speak to her, but at the same time he was concerned if he would probably further make her more nervous than she already appeared.

He finally decided to quench his confusion and got up from his seat and turned towards her, he did not take a step closer, fearing that his move might signal something otherwise or could possibly frighten the young lady. The first glance he had of her; he went completely awestruck. She looked like a sight to behold, it was hard not to notice her large expressive eyes, which were trying to escape his gaze and were looking either down or around as though her eyes were trying to tell a story of her own waiting to be interpreted. Her long, lustrous hair shimmered in the soft breeze, while each silky strand swayed gently, as if serenading the air itself. Some locks danced playfully around her face, teasing and tantalizing her, which she would friskily try to tuck behind her ears. He couldn't take his eyes off her and couldn't help but admire her.

Zunaisa was equally puzzled, astonished, and confused all at once; her cheeks were flushed as she tried to escape his sharp gaze which she could sense was fixed right on her. She gathered herself, cleared her throat and then looked up at him. Their eyes met, for the first time and everything around seemed to have taken a halt. It was as though the time froze and their eyes were locked to each other. That one moment of gaze oozed intense passion and longing, it felt as though fate designed their meeting in an unmatched perfection straight out of a fairy tale waiting to be a story which history would talk about.

"Umm, hi, I am Paras. Nice to meet you, uhh, Miss?" His eyes were still hooked to hers, not in a manner that would make someone uncomfortable but his gaze depicted a longing to know her more. He couldn't help but notice how the glistening moonlight complemented her red dress and the pearl neckpiece she was wearing. Her chocolaty and dusky complexion was luminous, her skin visibly glowing in the darkness; soft and supple. To him, she was like a season of spring, full of vibrant colours and undeniable charm.

Zuanisa, on the other hand, was just as captivated. She noticed his eyes, which had a peculiar shine. Even in the shadows, she could see that they were not entirely black but carried hues of grey and hazel. He was tall, well-built, and sporting a rugged stubble that perfectly complemented his chiselled jawline.

"Uhhh! Hi Paras, my name is Zunaisa Rizvi. It is nice to meet you too." Her nervousness and shyness could very well be deciphered in her tone of voice, which she tried hard not to project. "I am sorry to have startled you. I was just given some dare by my friends to find someone and speak to that person, and I was just trying not to be a spoilsport and willingly agreed to do this." Zunaisa kept on talking and explaining how things had transpired and how she ended up finding him sitting here while Paras's eyes were glued to her, her expressions and her eyes, he couldn't help but admire her talk. He soon realized that she was more than just a pretty face and had so much more to her, her personality spoke a story of its own. Then something struck him. He comprehended that he had been noticing her for far too long and thought that he might really catch her off guard, therefore, he broke his silence finally. "Your friends do seem to be a lot of fun, and might I say, how you sportingly took the dare, speaks to me that you are pretty brave. If I were at your place, I would probably have been scared for my life thinking it must be a mountain ghost or something and would have run for my life." They both chuckled at Paras's humour.

"So, are you here alone for an escapade, or are you accompanied by someone? Although, now that I am here, I feel like this can be a fantastic spot to just pack your bags and take a retreat alone," Zunaisa said. By now her nervousness had receded, she was able to be herself and was a tad bit comfortable around him. "Yeah! Umm, I am here with my friends although my lot is pretty boring unlike yours, they all were rolled up in bed before 9pm and are very excited for the hike in the morning. I was just having a hard time falling asleep, mountains aren't really my thing. I am more of a beach person I think; mountains are good for these hopeless romantics and lovers, but it's definitely not my cup of tea, well, that's that, and so I decided to take a brief walk before I hit the sack. Tell me more about you, Zunaisa."

As he spoke, Zunaisa also kept looking at him, enjoying the conversation they were having. While they were talking, he gestured to her to sit next to him, and she hesitantly agreed. However, she wasn't too happy to find out that he wasn't fond of the mountains whereas she was an ardent lover of the mountains, the mountains rejuvenated her mind and her soul. But in her mind, she tried to debate that two people with opposite interests could also get along and the other half of her mind was fighting her as to why she was paying so much attention to the likes and dislikes of a stranger she just met. "I love the Mountains, I think the nature around you pushes you to feel your feelings, feel the freshness and fall in love with it. I mean not that I take it away as to how fun beaches can be, but Mountains will have my unprecedented admiration." She smiled as she looked at him, and he smiled back at her. The unexpected encounter was now possibly heading towards a brimming and blossoming of something great.

They kept on talking, totally engrossed in each other, they were enjoying each other's company and as the night grew darker the temperature started falling too, she tried to almost hug herself to keep warm; he on the other hand despite how much he wanted to hold and hug her tightly so she wouldn't feel cold; couldn't do it. So, finally, he decided to take off his sweatshirt and gave it to her, "Here, Zunaisa, please take this. This will keep you warm, else I am afraid you might fall sick."

Paras was rather stoic, he never believed in romance or fairy tale love stories, it was his conditioning as a man that he must always be strong and that being expressive was a feminine trait to him, since he was the only son in the family and had three sisters; his household functioned in a strict patriarchal setup. He was taught to always take the lead, reason things and to use his mind over his heart. But in that moment with Zunaisa, Paras felt as though he was unknotting a new side of him, he was taken aback by what was happening to him around her presence, in his head there were whirling waves of thoughts; he wasn't able to understand as to why was he unable to resist not being expressive towards this girl he just met.

What was fate trying to do? He kept questioning it but at the same time his heart felt a sense of solace that he hadn't experienced in a very long time, it was as though he could speak to her for hours. Zunaisa too, wanted the time to just freeze there and then so they could spend the whole night talking and gazing into each other's eyes. To her, this was a type of an encounter that was something she always thought about in her imagination, and she was thrilled to see it manifest in her real life.

She took his sweatshirt and placed it on her lap. They discussed a few stories from school and college. Paras had already graduated from law school and was now working as a lawyer in one of the most reputed law firms in Delhi whereas Zunaisa was still in her fourth year of law school trying to explore, find her niche and learn more. Paras was a very silent and introvert guy, he barely liked to make friends whereas Zunaisa on the other hand was quite a social butterfly, she was supremely active in extracurricular activities and loved to talk and uncover new interests. But somehow, in spite of all the contrasts they did seem to have; they were happy to find some common ground since they both shared the same professional background, and to them, the connection just felt right. Their opposites were surely attracting and balancing their chemistry.

Their conversation was interrupted when they heard some footsteps across the pavements and some distant chatter of a couple of people. They both were astonished and started wondering who they could be.

"Oh wait, guys, guys, I see her, she is here, OH MY GOD ZEEEE! Have you lost your mind? Where have you been? We all got so worried for you." Ritu ran to her and hugged her. Rey, Shanaya and Urvi followed. "I kept telling Prakriti that this dare was a pathetic idea but you guys wouldn't listen, we almost had a heart attack and we weren't able to find you Zunaisa." She hugged them all and reassured that she was fine, then Rey intervened, visibly annoyed and sceptical, to find a man standing beside her sister. Rey tried hard not to lash at him, his brotherly instincts had kicked in, "And may I know who this gentleman is? Excuse me, Mister, may I know who you are?" Rey gave a point-blank straight face to Paras as though he just wanted to rip him apart at his audacity to come close to his beloved sister.

Zunaisa sensed that Rey was practically pissed at him as he was extremely protective and before things took a bad turn, she jumped in to introduce Paras to everyone. She briefly apprised everyone how she met him and how he sportingly took the dare. She apologised to everyone for being a trouble as she lost track of time and nudged everyone that they all should head back to their bonfire and resume the game. "Well thank you Paras, I am sure you had to bear her talk and yap all along which is quite a task," Shanaya laughed and others did too.

"Actually, I wouldn't have liked to spend my night any other way than to hear her talk." Paras's eyes gleamed and smiled as he looked at her. Zunaisa blushed, the chemistry and the tension brewing between them was outpouring and loud that one could sniff even from afar; the girls couldn't help but smile and chuckle. "I suppose, this is enough girls, we should get back now, it's getting late." Rey staunchly imposed that the girls march back quickly and did not give much time to Zunaisa either, so that she could at least bid him a goodbye.

Rey tucked Zunaisa over the shoulders and they started heading to the bonfire site, while Paras kept on looking at them as they slowly walked away. Zunaisa even though did not want to leave but had no choice but to go back with everyone, she felt as though she was living a beautiful dream and just then someone woke her up, she could do anything to go back in time and relive those moments she spent with him. Paras was a little remorseful too. He too wanted her to stay and talk the whole night with her and watch the sunrise, but it seems all good things do not last as long as we like. He just hoped that she would at least turn one last time before he finally loses her sight.

She turned back one last time to look at him, his heart skipped a beat and he bid her a good bye with a faint smile and a heavy heart with the hope to see her again soon.

THE DREAM GIRL

Back at the bonfire sight, there was a lot of commotion and chit chat all around. They all swarmed and bombarded Zunaisa with a lot of questions out of their excitement and inquisitiveness. All the girls were dying to know who this guy was; was it a start of something romantic or was it just a random interaction that might barely last long, the group was totally all in to find out all the details of the mysterious meeting Zunaisa had. While they were engrossed in their conversation, it soon started to get close to sunrise, so they all decided to wait a bit longer to watch it before heading back to their rooms.

That morning the sun looked radiant and appeared in a shade of red and yellow, the morning breeze was fresh and moist, the atmosphere was surreal and surrounded by the hymns of different birds singing, chirping in a melodious tune, as though they were signalling the onset of a new day, a new beginning and new opportunities ready to be unfolded. They all soaked up the view and then retreated to their respective rooms.

Everyone was tucked into their beds except Zunaisa who was tossing and turning restlessly on her bed having a hard time falling asleep. She couldn't help but aimlessly think about the engulfing encounter she had with Paras; it was as if she would pawn all that she had to relive that one moment with him but alas! It felt that the moment went by like quicksand. She kept wondering if he was also thinking about her, what were the odds she would bump into him again? She barely knew his full name or a possible way to contact him. She whispered a prayer to God that may He reunite them both again, and with that, she shut her eyes and went off to sleep.

"Bro, I cannot believe you did not ask her for her phone number. I mean the chances of meeting such a pretty girl at such a secluded place are next to impossible and you just wasted a God's given opportunity, we have to find her for him boys," Yuvi said. Paras and his friends: Anirudh, Utkarsh, and Yuvi were hiking the valley across which had a small adjacent remote village called "Kumati", in Uttarakhand.

Uttarakhand was a popular go-to tourist spot for everyone living in and around Delhi owing to its proximity and easy accessibility. The boys had decided to spend their short winter break there. Considering how cold it gets in December in the mountains, the footfall of the area was lesser than usual, the freezing temperatures and offbeat retreat were something only a few cherished.

Paras, was equally upset, thinking why did he not muster the courage to ask her for her phone number. The meeting with her was playing on his mind on loop, he hadn't felt so strongly for someone in a very long time. But at the same time, he was trying to resist his urge of thinking about her. It was as though he was fighting a losing battle: a battle between his head and heart, wherein the brain tries to reason every situation, and the heart just wants to wander and just be, superseding any logic or rationale.

Interestingly enough, the heart always comes out victorious, more likely so when it is pitted against our minds in matters of love. Love conquers all rationality, and the heart follows a tune and path of its own without much ado, but that is, if you really truly feel those butterflies and gleam for someone.

Soon he realized that there was no point in trying to deny what he was feeling, he was certain that these feelings aren't just out of the blue and they are deeper than he himself could fathom. He decided to surrender and not self-sabotage something so endearing that he had felt and found. Paras was now beginning to lament his loss contemplating as to why he did not make the most out of this once in a lifetime opportunity. However, despite the odds and the unfavourable circumstances he wasn't completely hopeless, he was certain that he would meet her again.

"The force that made us meet and brought her into my life will reunite us again," he muttered while looking up in the sky as though he was just trying to reassure his heart and himself. The lines on his forehead were tense, he rather seemed in a pensive mood and was looking at the sky and around, just mumbling to himself. Anirudh sensed that even though Paras is physically here and trying his best not to show his emotions, an art Paras mastered; he knew his friend needed a shoulder to lean on and confide in. Anirudh casually nudged him in order to reassure him, he was Paras's closest friend since childhood, Paras always felt at ease around him and never hesitated in embodying his vulnerability in front of him. He was aware of Paras's childhood, his conditioning at home and how the situations always pushed him further into a shell of his own where he would only allow a handful to enter.

Paras had a tough childhood; he was brought up in an abusive and dysfunctional home. His father was a hard-liner who believed that the men of the house were superiors and women were made solely for catering to the needs of the household. Paras's father wasn't an ideal father after all, his ideologies were apparently slightly more male-dominant and he frequently regurgitated his superiority through his actions, whether it was handling the finances or seeking permission to do any chore. He established himself as the supreme and nobody ever dared to question him. His father was also involved in multiple extramarital affairs and would often be physically abusive towards his mother, he would return from work and would beat her mother every single night. Sometimes, the bruises were so severe that his mother could barely move or speak the next day but her mother bore all of the abuse with patience and a smile just for the sake of her children.

A mother's love is nonpareil, the sacrifices a mother makes since she conceives the baby, to the delivery and the weaning of the child, are a series of labour and pain which only a mother can relate to and understand. Paras loved and respected his mother but somehow as a kid he slowly started to create walls around himself, he started to feel that somehow it was his mother's fault that she couldn't keep his father happy as he would often overhear his father complaining and nagging how his mother wasn't pretty enough and did not make an effort to look good for her husband.

The nascent years of a child hold extreme significance and childhood trauma many a times manifests as real-time personality disorders and other mental health issues which most of us often either overlook or leave undetected; and lead our lives with a broken-spirit. However, from time to time these traumas resurface and hinder our everyday lives and our interpersonal relations.

Paras was a victim of it too, he was a victim of an unhappy home and parents who never saw real love and hence, gradually he developed an introverted disposition; suppressing his feelings and perhaps subconsciously he even started to accept his father's ideologies that men are the stronger beings and need to channelise their dominance in every walk of life. Somewhere deep down, he had accepted that the kind of relationship his parents share is normal and that is how ideally every couple is or should be. Consequently, he succumbed to many failures in establishing any kind of intimate relationship and if at all he did make any connection it did not last long because the times were rapidly changing and evolving. The society was now more open to female counterparts and they were revered and valued which somehow contradicted the belief system that Paras upheld since childhood. He was beginning to realise that his current feelings colluded with his already set principles but this time he wanted to fight his way through and embrace the unknown.

"It is alright Paras, you will find her soon, I can see how much she has consumed you. I can see the sparkle you have for her in your eyes, something which I never saw before," Anirudh said and gave him a reassuring side hug. "Yeah bro, I have to find her! You are right I have never felt this before and if I don't, I would be disappointed in myself; now enough of this icky one on one talk. Back off now! For I fear that you might end up kissing me, haha!" They both burst into fists of laughter and galore. The boys then continued their hike around the village and decided to stay for lunch to try the local cuisine and soak in the view.

Kumati was a hidden gem, it was a small settlement with close to only 40-50 tiny huts and buildings, but despite being a tiny settlement it surprisingly had a school and a local dispensary or a *hakimkhana* as the locals called it. The boys were amused to find a school, a tiny playground with few swings and a see-saw, they decided to hog onto the swings and relive their childhood. They were having the time of their lives; it was as if they were back in school and there was nothing to worry about. They played and ran like a bunch of kids, living to every bit like there is no tomorrow. All they knew was that they were making memories that would brighten their days each time they would reminisce about it.

On an altitude as high as 6000 feet, everything around had a natural allure. The boys just couldn't help but gasp at the sunset, uncanny to their behaviour but it was spectacular, one could barely resist to not look at it and admire the beauty of nature. It was probably a first for Paras too, he never thought of gazing at the sunsets or the moon, but that day it felt that the sun and the sky were particularly dipped in the shades of love, with all the red, pink and yellow hues, it was beyond perfect. The stunning view reminded him of Zunaisa. She was all of that to him, a beautiful, enthralling ray of light shining back at people.

They then wandered around the school building, the school had fairly decent infrastructure, benches, water coolers, etc. They saw some interesting wall-art which apparently seemed hand-painted by the students, they were in awe of the place.

Just then their commotion was interrupted by an old lady who was the native of that place; her name was *Tulu Amma*, she was dressed in a local traditional attire, it was a vibrant saffron saree tied and draped around her neck in a halter style. *Tulu Amma* would carry a long stick with her to help navigate and support her while walking up the uneven surface, she would occasionally swing it to control her herd of sheep which she took for a daily walk for grazing around the valley. She was the wife of the village Sarpanch who graciously invited the boys to stay the night over at her place and enjoy the enriching heritage of Kumati. The boys were thrilled with the unexpected invitation, they thought, what could be a better way to explore an offbeat village than to spend time with the actual natives and learn about their rich history, cuisine and customs.

Tulu Amma had arranged a gathering with lots of native food and music in honour of her guests. The boys were welcomed with trumpets, drums and garlands, it was an overwhelming experience for them. There was a huge bonfire in the middle of the gathering and all the natives were sitting across it, some of the natives were performing their local folk dance and others had interesting folklores to tell. The dishes were simply delectable, even the plain rice and pulses tasted way better than what they would have in the cities. They were served fish, prawns, and some unique pickles which were made out of vegetables like beans, carrots, etc. The boys also contributed and shared their experiences about the cities, it was a healthy exchange of cultures between them.

The kids of the village were excited to meet the boys and insisted that they play some games and take a night hike around the valley, as they could likely spot some wild animals on their way. They all went out for a small walk before calling it a night as they had to head back to Delhi the following morning and settle their dues with their hotel before they could leave. The boys had a lot of fun, moving around with the kids who had so much to talk about and share. *Tulu Amma* came looking out for them as it was getting really dark and wasn't safe for them to be out at this hour. They all retraced their way to the village and called it a night.

Back in the hut, everyone quickly went off to sleep since they were all pretty exhausted. But Paras on the other hand, wasn't able to sleep, even though he had such a fun day, he was somehow still feeling empty, as if something was missing; it was a hollow feeling that he just wasn't able to comprehend. His heart was whispering to him and yearning, deep down he knew that it was for Zunaisa. "As soon as I reach Delhi, I will do whatever it takes to find her. Something tells me that she isn't that far, I will move heavens and the earth for you Zunaisa, and this time I wouldn't let you go." Paras affirmed himself.

The following day, the boys got up early since they had to hike back all the way to their hotel and leave Uttarakhand for Delhi. They thanked and hugged *Tulu Amma* and everyone in the village for their great hospitality. It was an hour's hike back to the hotel, the boys bid their goodbyes and flocked towards their pavilion. Yuvi and Utkarsh, was also equally aware that their boy had fallen hard for this girl and on their way back they had decided that they would help Paras find the love of his life, thinking that the stakes were high and Paras being the guy he was, he might not actively seek or express his feelings to her so they must act on the situation and help him. When they reached the hotel, they all decided to have their breakfast there; and shortly thereafter, they would head to their rooms to pack up their belongings.

"Rajesh, Brother!! Please understand our boy is in love after a long time and we really need to find her. I am afraid if we don't, we shall be cursed on behalf of these lovebirds," Yuvi said. "Sir, please understand it is the Hotel's policy, we cannot hand over the guest's details like that to you, doing this can land us into trouble," the manager said. "Our brother Paras, is actually sick and he might have only a few days left with us, his last wish is to find this girl we just want to honour his last wish as his friends," Yuvi retorted dramatically. Utkarsh looked at Yuvi, surprised and shocked to see how he was making things up just to get those details, he did feel he went out of the line but at the end of the day they were doing it for a good cause so he pitched in too. They were finally instrumental in their persuasion. The manager, Mr. Rakesh, although he did not dispense all the information, but did give them her full name. They thanked him and quickly left to join others at the breakfast table by the poolside.

Anirudh and Paras were already sipping on their coffee and enjoying some freshly cut fruits, Yuvi and Utkarsh joined them with faces all lit up. "Aren't you two a little too chirpy for the morning?" Paras said. "Well, if you hear what we are about to tell you, you might just be twice as chirpy or maybe scream at the top of your lungs," Yuvi winked. "Oh! Come on, let us not beat around the bush, our boy has anyway waited for far too long, let us just tell him already. Paras, the name of your dream girl is ZUNAISA RIZVI," Utkarsh said with all the enthusiasm and euphoria.

Paras couldn't believe what he heard; God really did hear his silent prayers. He couldn't believe his friends went through all the pain for him. He almost screamed out of happiness and hugged them both. "You have no idea how much this means to me; I mean, I now finally feel that there is a hope that I can find her," his eyes were emanating sheer happiness and gratitude. It was a great start for the day for him, the boys were exhilarated too. Paras couldn't wait to get back to Delhi and further his quest to find the girl of his dreams. The boys then dived into their breakfast buffet and savoured the pancakes, waffles, croissants and freshly pressed juices before heading back to their rooms for a check out.

It was the last day of their trip and it was ending on such a high note for them. Paras was convinced that this trip is going to be a memory of a lifetime for him; etched in his heart forever.

WHEN I SEE YOU AGAIN

"*It feels like the hills have embraced me; I feel the warmth even though the breeze is cold... You are not here but your presence is all I feel...*" with a sigh she wrote it down in her diary; perhaps it was a deliberate attempt to lighten her heavy contemplation and wiring thoughts. She wondered if this is what lovers feel and talk about, an unconditional, unpredictable, unprecedented series of emotions that catch you when you least expect it. A lurking feeling that compels you to feel and believe that you know this person since forever, that you would break through all the insurmountable odds just to be with this person and all their flaws begin to seem flawless to you.

The vibe of the bachelorette gang was spiking with feelings of joy and happiness, the girls were having a gala time. They were all seated around the poolside for a sumptuous brunch and soaking in the sun. "Still waiting for your prince charming to show up randomly? You have to take efforts to find him, he just wouldn't pop up randomly like that in front of you," Shanaya told Zunaisa. "You are being ridiculous. I am not thinking about him, I was just wondering and planning all that I have to do once I get back to Delhi, I have to even send the wedding invites and there is so much on my plate already," Zunaisa protested as sternly as she could. She couldn't let her guard down so easily in front of everyone, not even Shanaya for that matter. But she knew that her words were defying what she was truly feeling from within, she was just hoping for a miracle to happen so that he may somehow find her and this time she wouldn't let him go.

"Now please would you give me a moment? My girl gang is on the hotline dying for me to spill the beans and pour the tea for them," she smirked. Shanaya sportingly took her request to let her have her time with her friends. Meanwhile, she got connected to her best friends Monica, Annie and Apala, on a video call; they all were friends since childhood or as long as they could remember, their friendship practically grew up with them. These girls were inseparable, sharing every bit of their lives, understanding and supporting each other despite their diverse professional fields and circumstances; they all shared one thing in common and that was their love for each other.

Monica was a recruiter in human resources and a key team member at a leading MNC, Annie was a student of literature and a budding make-up artist, and Apala was an extremely talented art director, with movies was her first love. Although all four of them came from a different background, different work profiles, their love for each other was transcendent, cherubic and pure; they would stand and support each other through thick and thin. These girls would flock together back in the school days, however, as much as they would have loved to be around each other as often as they could; their work life and other personal goals turned their get togethers into episodes of meeting maybe quarterly in a year.

Nonetheless, they would keep each other informed about their lives, their work or whatever it is that they would like to share. Some days, their discussions would be reminiscing about high school days, their first bunks, their first crushes, and on certain days when life would cast an unsettling and not-so-comfortable experience, then they would create a safe space for themselves to discuss and vent all the bottling feelings and emotions out.

As much as the world is constantly involving there are few things which remain constant since the inception of humankind, for instance here, the womenfolk feel better when they vent out their emotions and do not necessarily try to logic everything or try to salvage the situation; but men more likely so want to fix every hurdle or any problem that comes to them. Indeed, God created a man and a woman significantly different but somehow the harmony lies in accepting those differences to form authentic connections.

Zunaisa felt much more at ease sharing her vulnerabilities with them rather than her male friends, not because they would not care for her but sometimes; all a person needs, is someone to just listen to them. Annie, Monica and Apala were her safe space and these girls would really move the mountains to uplift each other, their friendship was truly organic and unparalleled.

Zunaisa finally broke the news of meeting Paras. Her friends were thrilled to know that their best friend had finally met someone she strongly feels for. She knew they would never outrageously judge her for her feelings; while they would reprimand her, should she need it, but they did give her the liberty to be herself and speak her heart out.

"Tell us more about him, what does he look like? I mean a tall, mysterious handsome guy and you guys randomly meet at a hilltop? Damn! I can barely control my excitement; this feels and sounds surreal. You have to go find him, girl! I will help you stalk him on social media; you know how savvy I am in that," Apala retorted with all her exuberance and enthusiasm.

"Well, not really, Apala, if what Zee says is true and if he also feels for her, he should have found a way to contact her by now, I don't think Zee should be the first one to initiate, his lack of efforts possibly shows his lack of interest, she cannot be putting herself like that in front of him," Monica spoke outrightly. "Monica is right, she must not let history repeat itself," Annie intervened. As Annie spoke, the situation and the air around the conversation turned rather tense, Annie somehow unconsciously opened a box of memories Zunaisa possibly wasn't ready to unravel yet. She did understand that her friends were just coming from a place of concern and were trying to protect her from yet another heartbreak. Her friends and family very well knew that Zunaisa was a giver and often her energy and emotions were wrongfully capitalised on by people. It was hard for her well-wishers to not relate to what had happened to her in her past relationship with Aditya.

Aditya was a significant part of her life; the first to awaken feelings she had never known before, her first love since childhood. We all know the feeling that the first love comes with; it always remains special and is etched in our hearts and minds almost for our whole lives. First love is often associated with true innocence and sincerity. It is for the first time that a human heart understands the complexities of emotions it can have or feel for someone they may not be directly related to. The possibilities and the stratospheric levels of emotions that come by in a whirlwind are thoroughly a kind of feeling and experience which makes the person realise that they have a heart, and it has a definite way of exuding emotions other than the logical side of the brain.

First love is an experience that everyone goes through and it steadily grows on you. It gives us a realisation that love transcends boundaries, it is beyond the limitations and plausible human constraints that exist in the world; love operates on its own laws. There is no hard and fast rule in love that a person must or ought to fall in love at a particular age, time, person, ethnicity or any other boundaries that happen to exist. Anybody could fall in love with anyone when they least expect it or with someone, they always had a liking for; whether or not that love materialises into a long-lasting one is a touché but a lover always holds his love in esteem and craves a loving forever with them.

First love and the experiences associated with it build a strong foundation for our future relationships. We tend to learn about the embodiments of human emotions, tolerance and much more. We get to learn and understand to peacefully co-exist even if our interests don't match and sometimes, we learn bitter lessons in life like permanence is a false notion or that one should know how to set standards for oneself and not let the other walk all over them. Be as it may, the depth and significance the first love holds in a person's life remains unmatched. It is truly one-of-a-kind feeling; our emotions are spiking, we are full of zest, and possibly ready to put everything at stake just for that one love.

However, as much as we like our first love to materialise in a lifetime commitment, it more often than not doesn't last forever, as we would have essentially daydreamed. In fact, you would seldom find it lasting forever, and even though it may not last as long, it surely does teach us life lessons. You grow as a stronger person and understand that you cannot get way too complacent even though you might be loving that person with all your heart, putting anybody on a pedestal way too high becomes a reason for your own downfall.

It wasn't that Aditya was the wrong guy for her but one could say he was perhaps in her life at the wrong time. The giver that Zunaisa was: the vibrant teenager that she was, she would go all in for him to ensure Aditya feels loved and pampered. She would write him letters, songs, make him handmade cards. She would always make sure she was available for him when he called her at any given time despite her schedule. Aditya would often show his concern thinking that she was investing too much of her time in him, they both shared a considerable age difference, and he soon decided to end the relationship on an abrupt note. She was devastated, she felt abandoned, she tried her best to reason with his sudden decision. Her logical mind was just having a tough time accepting why he would decide to leave her even though she was giving her all to him, it took her years to understand only after as an adult that the breakup was for her own good, it was rather a breakthrough for her to become a more refined maiden and that there was possibly no future; sometimes loss is a greater gain. She was way too involved with him, forgetting that she had a world of her own. His choice, even though as one sided or selfish it might have looked to her back then, it was a blessing in disguise for her.

But even though we humans have been blessed with the ability to train our minds to forget things and move on, the heart clings on to certain episodes of emotions, feelings, people and relationships. She had unconsciously developed a feeling of abandonment and therefore, tried her best to safeguard all her relationships and give in more than anyone would without expecting much in return. She would feel a burnout at times but then the thought of service and being able to help the people she cares about or even in general made her feel accomplished. Even though her first relationship wasn't exactly what she wanted it to be, she did fondly recall the moments she spent with him, and years later, she finally felt that she would like to venture into a possible blooming romance, and this time better attuned to her individuality and a sense of purpose that this relationship would last.

She was always the type to believe in long fulfilling love and relationships. She wanted to have a family of her own, children and a nice cosy place she would call home; even though her desires seemed conventional to many given that she was looked on as a driven individual and admired for it too. She would never shy away in embodying her true essence or feelings which is what made her truly authentic and charming. She would be the most real person in the room and would never hesitate in expressing herself even at the cost of being judged for it or not matching the general consensus. Zunaisa couldn't wait to start her journey with Paras.

Everyone had their fair share of opinion and were projecting their discernment over the whole situation, they were concerned that what if she gives in more efforts than him, what if he tries to take undue advantage of her fragile behaviour and coins on that, but Zunaisa was convinced that what they both experienced: was a feeling which seemed to be transcending the physical realms, merging the two souls into a union, unique to their own. It was as if the union and the outpouring influx of emotions could only be understood and felt by the only ones experiencing it.

She knew she had to step out of her whimsical world or else everyone would just be worried for her. She did not wish to spoil her sister's bachelorette and make the trip about her. Therefore, Zunaisa in her classic attempt cracked some jokes to divert the attention, she just knew how to bring up the energy and the mood of the room she would be in. She wanted everyone to enjoy themselves and not be ruminating about her much doleful plight. Zunaisa hung up the group call on a chirpy note and promised her friends with more updates once she gets back.

She then shook her head and decided to live in the moment and not to think much about the things she had no control over. Time surely does passes by in a jiffy when you are surrounded with people you care about; therefore, she wanted to make the most of this trip and spend time with her best friend, her darling Shanaya and her dearest brother Rey. She walked back to the poolside where everybody was soaking in the sun, dancing and enjoying their lunch, she was happy to see everybody having the time of their life and she too, wanted to be present in the moment and enjoy every bit of it while it lasts.

You see, the more we seem to care about things the more it tends to slip away, so it is always better to let things be and if it is meant for us then nothing in this world can stop it from happening or reaching to us. What is meant for you will reach you even if it were on the opposite ends of the Earth and what isn't meant for you, you wouldn't be able to catch hold of it even if it were placed on your palms.

As much as Zunaisa wanted to shun away her thoughts and be focused in the present, it was hard for her to not flog the dead horses and find answers to all her questions and doubts. She was also slowly getting more desperate and anxious contemplating if he was also equally thinking about her, or if was he also wondering that there could be a way they could connect again. It had been days since that encounter happened, and she hadn't heard from him. There was a tempest of emotions all around her; although she was a master at helping people solve their most complex problems with such ease, she struggled to deal and keep up with her problems and emotions.

It wasn't that she was unaware of her anxiety, she recognised it early on even when she was a kid, she was aware that she did have severe anxiety and extreme situations did take a toll on her mental health, there were times she experienced panic attacks; no matter how much things like anxiety, depression etc were considered a taboo, she never hesitated in acknowledging it. Almost every other person has anxieties and other mental health issues and the first step to cure the issue is to first have the ability to acknowledge and accept it without fearing the judgment of society. She was lucky to have friends and family who understood her anxiety and were always on the lookout to help her whenever she would feel overwhelmed.

It was around five in the evening and everyone was slouching and taking a moment to slow down and unwind after the poolside party had ended. Now, they just wanted to relax and savour the high tea, enjoying the chill of the temperature and being snuggled with their warm cup of tea; an exquisite blend of comfort and calm.

Zunaisa took a high chair that was neatly placed at the rooftop restaurant of the property. The restaurant was serving all kinds of cuisines for the comfort of the guests as the market was many miles away from it, the rooftop had an overlooking view of the mountain ranges and tiny distant settlements spread across. Few villagers carried wood logs on their back and some walked back to their homes with their herd of sheep and goats; a sight which one could barely find in the big cities. As she took in the view, her phone beeped, there was a notification on her Instagram handle. She picked up her phone to check it, her heart racing and pounding in anticipation if it was Paras, she hurriedly scrolled through her message section.

But alas, she was disappointed to see it was just another spam message. It was coming to dawn upon her that perhaps Paras was just a dream, too good to be true. But she was an ardent and fierce lover, she knew that she wouldn't give up on someone she truly felt for. It wasn't necessary that a man had to take the first step, in her head she thought what if he wanted her to take the first step. She had too many doubts and just when she thought of putting her phone away, she saw another message pop up; to her utter dismay, it was yet another spam message, given that her social media handle was a public profile and she would actively post about her life and other related content, she naturally received thousands of messages and notifications but her eyes were looking for that one person in the pool of thousands and as much as she hoped it was him, he was still nowhere to be found.

She couldn't deny that from the deepest pit of her heart she wanted him, not just as a friend she knew she wanted more. Zunaisa whispered her prayers to God, she was having a feeling as though she had finally met the man of her dreams and was on cloud nine. Just the thought about him made her feel like she was the luckiest girl to have ever existed. She somehow felt and knew that something great and grand awaits; she had a firm belief that God would reunite them soon, in fact in a much better way than she could imagine or plan. The trip was about to get over, and they were all set to go back to Delhi. She knew the memories she had made on this trip were going to be engraved in her heart for years to come.

THE BEAUTIFUL GAME OF DESTINY

A warm, toasty sun caressed her cheeks, and the soft rays almost flashed at her closed eyes. She smiled and sniffed in the fresh, cool air and got off her bed. She slipped in her velvet slippers and walked up to the door-sized windows overlooking greenery all around and the gleaming sunrise curling over the city, the birds singing and some people jogging, others running their morning errands. The mornings in the cities were slightly different than the mountains, however the allure of the sunshine and the birds singing, remained the same throughout. Her heart was filled with excitement and happiness. Everything around looked and felt different and more beautiful than ever, she hadn't felt so alive ever. She smiled and thanked God to show her gratitude for the blessings she had and set her intentions for the day.

Zunaisa then quickly changed into her bathrobe and hopped into the shower to get ready for the big day. She was humming her favourite song out loud while the beautiful floral scent oozed out of her luxurious soaps and gels hovered around her room and the adjacent corridor.

She stepped out of the bathroom and picked out her uniform: a white crisp ironed top and tailored-made black pants and a mandatory black blazer.

There was something so powerful about this uniform, she felt empowered when she would wear it. She put on her uniform, combed her glistening and lustrous long hair into a sleek high ponytail; she then applied some lip stick which was of an old rose shade complementing her skin tone, along with that she wore her black stilettos and finally reached out to wear her signature cologne for her big day. She looked at herself in the mirror and said, "I cannot wait to put on my advocate's band and be a complete lawyer but for now my dearest Zee! We will have to wear our very favourite pearl piece," she smiled. The humming and the fragrance wrapping the air around signalled everyone in the house that Zunaisa was all set to leave; they were aware of her rituals of getting ready before stepping out. She thoroughly enjoyed dressing up, as if dressing up was her therapy. She loved to dress up, take care of herself, and invest a good amount of time in pampering herself; it was her form of self-love and expression, which she religiously followed and endeared.

Zunaisa's family was sitting around the dining table, enjoying some light and quick breakfast with some coffee and juices, discussing world politics, news about the country, and remunerating about some poems or poets, which was usually how they all started their day given that Zunaisa's father was a veteran in journalism who had dedicated more than four decades of his life to journalism, and her mother was a coveted poetess, super affluent in Urdu poems and shayaris. Zunaisa inherited cohesive qualities of creativity from her mother and hard work from her father. She adored and idolised her parents through and through, she shared a remarkably great bond with them and would discuss all spheres of her life with them. Rey had already left for work and Shanaya accompanied her parents at the dining table as she was an early bird and was super punctual with her timings. They all sat chit-chatting and waiting for Zunaisa to join them.

"Aquib, it is high time that you admonish and reprimand your beloved daughter. She is going to be fashionably late like always, and it's her first day at work. I just cannot believe this girl; I wonder why she takes such a long time to get ready," Zunaisa's mother told her father. Her father had a soft spot for her daughters, it was as if Shanaya and Zunaisa were the apple of his eye and he would give his all for them. "She is just a kid, Nikhat, relax, she will learn eventually. It is her first day so let us refrain from saying anything that might upset her," said her father.

"I cannot believe it is my first day of internship and I am already way too late than one could possibly or humanly be excused for, my boss might just fire me on my first day," Zunaisa panicked, while half-eating a slice of bread. She hurriedly started to pack her handbag and book a cab for herself to reach the High Court. "You are fashionably and religiously late at all occasions, and today is no different my dear, you are the sleepiest girl I know of. As a matter of fact, you wouldn't sacrifice your sleep even if you are held at gunpoint or if there is an earthquake too," her mother chuckled and reprimanded her. She was soon going to be a full-fledged lawyer now and being on time was an essential component of being a successful attorney.

"Mom, I love you but not right now please, I promise I will fix my sleep patterns and take you to places once I become the best attorney you have ever seen or known but for now just wish me luck and pray for my first day," she planted a kiss on mother's cheek, hugged her father and sister; and quickly hurried out of the house. She shared a friendly bond with her mother and, in general, with all her family members.

She hailed her cab and left for her destination. Delhi during the winters was a treat for everyone: the cold breeze brushing against your cheeks, sometimes a faint sun trying to cut through the dense fog and bring some relief to the inhabitants, and on other days, people would be blessed to experience clear skies and a sunny day.

The courts were situated in the vicinity of the VIP and diplomat areas, which were known to be one of the poshest areas of the city. The lush green pavements were decorated with various imported flowers like tulips, daffodils and cherry blossoms, to name a few, which were a treat and a delight for the onlookers to watch. Zunaisa was enjoying her short journey, the greenery and freshness were reminding her of the memorable trip she just had. Soon enough she reached the magnificent gates of the High Court; she took in the view not more than she could afford considering she was super late.

She rushed to the given court room number that was assigned to her a night before, where she was added in the official office WhatsApp group, the information was given to her via an anonymous number which she didn't really dare to pry much about and just begrudgingly took down the details even though in an ideal scenario she would cross question an anonymous number. In acute anticipation and nervousness of miserably failing to cast her great first impression she reached the given courtroom. She was trying to look for familiar faces and if not anyone at least her coveted senior whose chamber she had joined. To her utter misery she could barely find anyone other than the noise and chatter all around and the lawyers walking and rushing with their files and some clerks, interns and a few litigants following them.

She was scanning around the courtroom corridors, reading the space around, contemplating and imagining the day when she would become a lawyer and would hop from one court to the other for her matters. Revelling in the moment and almost losing herself in it, she was alarmed back to reality when someone nudged her shoulders. She gasped and turned around almost tip-toeing and slipping in shock as though someone woke her up from her daydream and before she could trip and fall, he gripped her tightly by the waist and held her in his arms.

She was flabbergasted and her eyes were wide open in shock, processing as to what had happened. She looked up into those hazel pairs of eyes which she recognised within seconds. They both looked at each other in such a way that it felt as though time had stopped and it was just the two of them looking into each other's eyes saying a lot without really saying anything at all. Suddenly it didn't matter where they were and who might be looking at them. The happiness gushing from their eyes was enough of a testimony itself.

He looked more handsome, gorgeous and appealing than she remembered, his strong muscular arms around her waist sent down chills to her spine. She couldn't help but notice how gorgeous his facial features were: those eyes, the dense eyelashes, the neatly combed hair, the tailored suit, and an ogling musk fragrance surrounding him were enough to cast a spell on anyone. Even in a crowd of thousands he would distinctly shine through.

Thereafter, she gathered herself and stood back up, he looked at her and smiled with all the love and affection, Zunaisa still pretty perplexed and almost bewitched by his beauty nodded and smiled back in response.

"What a pleasant surprise, Miss Rizvi! And my apologies for catching you off-guard like that. It seemed that you were pretty much lost in soaking your surroundings," Paras said. "Umm, yes, I mean no, I was not like daydreaming or anything, I was just, I mean, ugh. How are you here? What is happening? I don't know, I am super late for my first day here and I am mortified because I was supposed to be here by 10am and I am half an hour late, my boss will probably fire me and then I will fail this assessment internship and my dream of becoming a lawyer would go all go in vain." Zunaisa, almost being teary-eyed, started to vent out to Paras. He really wanted to hug and console her but he had to maintain the decorum of the court and tread the waters carefully. Therefore, he simply patted her shoulders gently to pacify her. "Well, well, I guess this might be your luckiest day because apparently your boss's instructions are that all the interns report to me. So, you don't really have to worry about being late, I will take care of it."

Paras had already discovered Zunaisa's name and other details during their trip, he would occasionally look at her profile on Instagram where she would post about herself, her life and her writings. He closely followed her and it was one of those days he found out that she was going to join the same office at which he works, as she posted about it on her social media. At that moment he came up with the idea to surprise her in person and welcome her as an intern there.

Zunaisa got further baffled than she already was, all of this was too much to comprehend. She first magically meets this guy she has been craving to meet for weeks, then she finds out he is a lawyer and not just any lawyer he is apparently her mentor at the firm she is supposed to work with. She tries to join the pieces in order to make sense out of the whole situation, but she could barely figure anything out. She felt happy, confused and curious all at once.

Paras sensed her heavy contemplation; her face was a canvas on which one could figure out all the emotions she might be feeling at the moment. He intervened and said, "Not everything can make sense all at once, shall we take one step at a time? We have one more matter at court room 16. The rest of the team is already there including sir. Let us join them, and you can observe the proceedings. Alright, Miss. Rizvi, shall we leave?" she nodded and followed him to court 16.

Paras expertly manoeuvred around the court like an expert; it seemed as though he was fully adept with the directions of the court premises, and he would occasionally exchange greetings with fellow lawyers. She was more impressed than ever when she saw all this, but she did not dare to express it but rather quietly observed and admired him. Soon, they reached their destination, and before walking inside, Zunaisa turned to Paras and said, "I am beyond happy and elated to see you here, I never thought I would find you again but I am glad we met again and we would be working together." He was equally happy and excited. "Likewise, I am happy to find you and I won't let you go this time. Now come on, let us hop in before we miss our turn," he replied.

They both entered and saw their senior sitting at the first row and reading on his files and a couple of people sitting behind him and their matter was about to be heard; Paras joined the others to brief the senior. Zunaisa stood at the back, diligently observing the court proceedings and her wonderment continued. Seeing a live Court proceeding was an enriching experience, she observed minutely how other lawyers argued and tried to make mental notes of it.

Their matter swiftly got over, and the whole team flocked together to head back to the office for other work that was assigned for the day. On the way back, Zunaisa ceased an opportunity to have a brief interaction with her senior which she thoroughly cherished and it filled her with zest to do more hard work and make a place of her own in the legal fraternity.

They reached their office; it was a boutique law firm with a clean and sharp interior. There were large volumes of books, files and bare acts, neatly placed over the shelves. It was a large space with cubicles and work stations for the associates and the interns to work on and adjacent to it was the conference room, a small pantry and followed by the main chamber of the Senior. She scanned the place around inquisitively, while the associates did not waste a single minute and sat in their respective cubicles and got buried in the large chunk of files to be read and worked on.

It seemed that the firm had a large volume of cases; given the expertise and eminence of her senior; it all made sense. The smell of coffee lingering around reignited her passion and confidence. She didn't want to waste a single moment, so she hurried to her seat to start the work that she would be assigned. She wanted to make the most of this internship; therefore, she started to read the files that were around and began making notes for herself.

She was glued to one of her files, reading everything attentively and taking down notes; just then she felt a hand brush against her gently. Surprised as she was, it was Paras, who sat next to her, watching with much enthusiasm as she read through the files, careful not to disturb.

Her beauty mesmerized him yet again; she looked like an art painted to perfection. He noticed how her lustrous locks would occasionally bother her, and she would tuck it to her earlobes every now and then. At times, she would pause, furrow her brows in concentration, and then she would nibble on to her pencil while taking down notes. The energy around her was simply contagious. He could watch her for hours but he couldn't control his fascination any further, therefore, he gently nudged her, "Haha! I love to startle you, by now I think I am an expert at it. You have been reading for such a long time that you did not realise it is lunch time already. Look around, everyone has left to grab something to eat," he said.

He did startle her yet again but she was somehow enjoying these sweet nothings and gestures. She smiled, "Absolutely, you are really great at freaking me out all the time, also I got so lost in my file that I lost track of time. Oh gosh! Everybody left and it is just the two of us now. Aren't you hungry?"

"I am famished Miss. Rizvi and I would love to buy some lunch and treat you with some awesome cheesecake that I know of around. Would you please join me? I would be honoured." He smiled and almost bowed at her, demonstrating utmost respect and chivalry. Paras was all that she ever dreamt of in a man, he was sharp, intelligent, chivalrous and good looking. This was all she ever wanted and her excitement skyrocketed, it was as if she was living her fairy tale romance that she always wanted. She grinned and responded, "Of course, I would love to join you. How could I say no to such a gracious and warm invite?"

They stepped out of their office, and while walking, he instinctively ensured that she was at the safer side of the road. When they reached his car; he held the door open for her and started to drive around smoothly ensuring that she felt safe. They both would occasionally steal glances at each other. There was something in the air around them, they both were aware but perhaps it was too soon to accept or acknowledge let alone express it to each other. They both wanted things to unravel at its pace. It seemed as though the anticipation and thrill that came with the tension when these two were around each other was fanning a possible blossoming romance.

Later that day, they sat together for lunch and by now the initial hesitation of not fully opening up or suppressing the urge to make eye contact had loosened up a tad bit. They both were getting comfortable with each other and started to genuinely enjoy being around one another. Their eye contact had now deepened and it was coupled with sheer laughter, jokes and banter; at times they were so loud that the people would look and stare at them with surprise and annoyance but they were too engrossed in each other to care or notice.

He felt alive like never before, and she, too, felt something deeper than ever before. They both were significantly different from each other. Paras was a reserved and introvert guy, and Zunaisa was a super friendly and extrovert girl. Yet, somehow, even in their differences there was mutual harmony and an unmatched symphony. It was as though their differences were only making them imperfectly perfect together.

During the ride back to the office, even though he was nervous, he mustered the courage and held her hand softly. To his surprise Zunaisa didn't resist and gently reciprocated the gesture. They kept holding hands throughout the drive while the cool breeze caressed their faces, and a cosy sun smiled at them. Paras noticed how Zunaisa's hair was dancing around with the breeze and the glistening golden rays of the sun were beautifully complementing her glass-like skin. She was a sight to look at, he would occasionally try to tuck back her locks softly while also stealing a few moments to affectionately brush his hands across her cheeks. He would notice that each time he would do this, she would blush and bite her lips in an attempt to stop herself from projecting her excitement but by now Paras could read past her silence; he knew she liked his soft touches and gestures. He knew she wasn't a girl who would allow anyone to come near her, let alone touch her, and perhaps, in her silence, there was a shared affection, which he could sense.

He was certain at this point that she trusted him which gave him butterflies, too; he was a completely different man in front of her. He was much more relaxed and composed, she gave him the peace and reassurance he always wanted or craved for. He saw the admiration she had for him in her deep profound eyes, he was happy that she could see through his tough exterior and genuinely appreciate and cherish him for his true authentic self. This engaging lunch date became a testimony that there was something more than just friendship or a mere encounter between the two of them. It was much more passionate, intimate, and deeper than it looked or they might have ever thought about. They both somehow knew that this ride back to the office is not the end, in fact it is a start to many more countless rides and moments to come forth.

They walk up to the office building holding hands, brushing against each other and exchanging all the banter and laughter but right before entering. Paras looked at her, "We are going to be working together now but we need to maintain some decorum in the office and around the team, it is not that I am afraid of anything but people do not shy away from gossiping and I do not want you to be a topic for unnecessary discussion." She nodded in agreement she was fully aware of the repercussions and took his words sportingly. She was aware that any adverse action or callous behaviour could cost her either losing the internship or be subject to unwarranted speculation which, she wasn't ready to face.

They enter inside successively and settle in their respective seats; Paras quickly went to his cubicle to prepare the drafts and briefs, while Zunaisa started to work on the files and research assigned to her by one of the associates.

The daylight would pass quickly during winters and it was an office protocol that all the female associates and interns must leave early and finish their work at home unless they would voluntarily like to either stay back or have something urgent that demands their presence at the office; they were free to go. On the other hand, the other associates had to be flexible with their timings, not that they had to work overtime, but if any discrepancy or situation arose, they had to step up and amend things.

It was quarter to eight and most of the associates began to log off and head back to their homes including Zunaisa. She knew that Paras would stay back for work, and, as much as she wanted to stay back, too, and if not anything but be able to seize a few more moments with him, however, much to her chagrin she couldn't. "Paras Sir? Since I have to report to you, I wanted to let you know that I am leaving. You can email me lest you need my assistance on anything. I will be available." This time she surprised Paras. He grinned and looked at her, almost shocked, but then he realised that, as an intern she was supposed to be report to him for everything, and as much as he wanted her to stay or drive her back home, his professional commitments kept his hands tied. His heart ached but he managed to serenade it by reminding that he would see her soon. He smiled and bid her goodbye and went back to his files.

"No way! I don't believe this; she is your intern? What is up with you two? This sounds magical. You two first meet each other in the mountains and then my friend you fall in love with her at first sight and now she is going to be working with you? I am happy beyond measure bro," Anirudh almost jumped in enthusiasm over the phone call. Paras answered, "Who said I am in love? It is too soon for that but yes, I do confess I like her, and while it sounds very exciting that I will be working with her, it might also get a little bit distracting for me to concentrate. I completely lose myself when I am around her. The way she smiles, her eyes speaks more than she does and the way she smells. She emanates everything of beauty and charm. How can I concentrate when she is working with me?" Anirudh laughed at his response "You tell me you don't love her and then speak about her like hopeless lovers do. Her eyes, smile, smell and what not. I kid you not bro, you never spoke like this even about Priya till date. But this girl? I am telling you; you can protest as much as you want but you are in love with her already, I can give it to you in writing."

Paras got a bit unsettled when he spoke about Priya. "She is nothing like Priya and please don't complicate things right now by comparing or mixing them together. I don't want to talk about it right now. I have to sleep. Go to sleep, Ani, bye," he hung up the call and left. However, Anirudh could read past his annoyance and silence like a pro, as much as he denied that he wasn't in love, he could fully comprehend that his best friend, his brother is head over heels for her. He had never heard him speak so highly about a woman, she brought a different side of him, his vulnerable and authentic self. Although Paras was not ready to speak or deliberate about the situation with Priya, but given how after such a long time, he was finally happy with Zunaisa; Anirudh decided to focus on this bond instead. He wanted to see his best friend happy and that is what mattered to him the most. He hoped that the two of them would get together and confess their feelings to each other soon but neither Paras nor Zunaisa were ready to either accept or to own those feelings yet.

Unlike Zunaisa, Paras wasn't that close to his family as much as he wanted to share the details about his day with his family, he just couldn't. He just mechanically followed a routine of heading back to home, freshening up, eating and straight away heading for his room. On some days he would be welcomed by his mother and on other days he would be welcomed by the squeaking noise of fighting and jibes of his parents and on those days, he would skip dinner and straight away retire to his room. But then he had Anirudh with whom he could share all of his day and life events. He was happier to have one genuine friend than to have ten friends or family members who just wouldn't genuinely care or bother. He believed in keeping his circle close and tight. He had a mantra: the less people you chill with, the less nonsense you have to deal with.

After he ended the call, he retreated to his bed, staring up at the ceiling and recalling the entire day: the conversations made, the moments shared, it all rolled up in front of his eyes like a movie. Soon enough sleep consumed him and he fell asleep.

TOGETHER IS MY FAVOURITE PLACE TO BE

He wakes up with a faint smile on his face and felt like everything around him was singing a tune of its own. The whole world felt different, a beautiful kind of different and liberating. These feelings were rather an unknown charter and realm but he willingly wanted to indulge and explore them. He just couldn't wait to see her, therefore, he quickly decided to get dressed up for the day and waste no time. He put in extra effort to get ready, he wanted to look the best for her. He never did something like this for anybody but with Zunaisa, he was ready to take the shots and put in the effort for her. To him Zunaisa was a beacon of hope and light in his mundane and otherwise gloomy and mechanical life. He never felt at ease at home and given his childhood and the allied dysfunctional family he came from; he would constantly seek solace and he found that in her. Zunaisa was not just any random girl in his life, she was more than he could possibly ever think of or express. He was happy to have finally found her.

Zunaisa was brimming with exuberance and happiness and everyone at home could sense her enthusiasm, she was up early and ready before time. Everyone at home, her parents and siblings were pretty surprised to see the sudden change of behaviour. "Wow... wow! Look who is up and all set to leave already? And you look surprisingly chirpier than ever. What's up Zee? Are you possibly sick? This can't be you," Rey teased her. She snapped at him "I just want to reach the Court on time. There is nothing new or different. Put a halt to your thoughts."

Her mother intervened, "Enough! You two stop this unnecessary bickering early in the morning. Rey, finish your breakfast quickly and Zunaisa, it is good that you are up early; try to keep up with this, for this will help you in the future. Now, no more dissing at each other, everyone can take care of themselves." Although Nikhat intervened to diffuse the jibe and bickering, she sensed that there was something going on with Zunaisa; this wasn't her usual behaviour. Her mother was a positive and vibrant lady who on any given day would appreciate her children for all that they would do; however, here, her motherly instincts kicked in which hinted that there was something behind the curtains.

Everyone left for their work and it was just Nikhat and Shanaya at the dining table. She looked at Shanaya who was smiling all along as though she was fully aware of the back story. Nikhat decided to confront her after

Zunaisa left. Shanaya at first tried her best to not to reveal much about what had transpired at the trip but to what extent could a child hide and conceal things from a mother? She was left with no choice; therefore, she reiterated the whole story to her mother. "Mom, she is a grown up now, you have to calm down there isn't anything to worry about. They briefly met there but I think they never met after that night. She did like him clearly but I don't think anything ever happened after that. Maybe she just took your advice seriously and wants to get to work on time. She won't do anything silly. I know her. You need to relax now." Nikhat got more concerned, she knew how fragile her daughter was, the thought of her being hurt by this man started to haunt her. What if Shanaya didn't know the whole story? What if they had met more than once, she pondered. She saw the glee in the eyes of her daughter which she had never seen before but she decided not to confront her yet and wait for her to come and tell her what was cooking behind after all. However, she urged Shanaya to speak to Zunaisa one on one and find out what was happening with her. Shanaya reassured her mother; thereafter, they both retreated to their respective work scheduled for the day.

There was a familiar looking tall and muscular guy standing with two cups of coffee to go in his hand skimming through and scanning the crowd as though he was trying to spot someone. As she walked closer to the man, it was none other than Paras. "Good morning, Mr.

Sethi. Looks like you are expecting someone?" He blushed and shook his head in agreement. "Yes, you are right, I was expecting you, Zunaisa. And I must say you look stunning in this uniform. Here! I got you some coffee. It will be a long day today and I thought you might need some dose of caffeine to go about the day." Her heart and mind started to dance and sway at his sweet gesture, she wondered how could a man be so gentle and caring.

After that, they both walked to the courtroom and realised that they were almost an hour early and had a significant amount of time to relax and unwind before the proceedings began. They sat at the waiting lounge discussing the matters that were listed for the day. Just then Siddharth walked in, "Hey Paras! How are you? You try to ignore me all the time brother but here I am. Haha!" Paras reluctantly hugged and exchanged pleasantries with him.

Siddharth was a hotshot lawyer of the High Court and was a senior to Paras in college. They never really got along and since Paras was an introvert, Siddharth would often mock or find ways to demean him back in college. But now that they both were practicing lawyers, the dynamics did change a bit but there still was some underlying bitterness. Paras always maintained his distance from him and spoke to him only when necessary.

Before Paras could say anything further, Siddharth's eyes got hooked to Zunaisa without waiting for Paras to introduce her. He walked up to introduce himself instead as he intended to instigate Paras yet again, "I have to say, I am yet to come across such a stunning lawyer. I believe we haven't met. I am Siddharth, Senior Associate at Jes Law." Zunaisa was slightly taken aback by the sudden compliment but she graciously responded. "Hello Sir! I am Zunaisa. That was very generous of you but I am an intern as of now. I work with Roy Sir and Paras Sir." He further deliberately responded in a more fashionable way per his usual responses. "We all were interns at one-point Zunaisa, you will be a very sharp lawyer I can tell." Before she could answer to him anymore, Zunaisa looked at Paras who was clearly flushed with anger, his face and in his eyes were bloodshot red. It was as though he was having such a hard time controlling his temper. Upon seeing Paras like that she decided not to engage any further in conversation with Siddharth and gestured Paras to walk away and thus the gathering dispersed.

Paras was fuming with anger and frustration; she was worried and a bit scared. It was the first time she was seeing this side of him. She was trying to gather and comprehend what exactly triggered him so much, was it because she spoke to him? Or that he complimented her? But why would he be affected at all? What were they anyway? They weren't in a relationship nor did they confess anything to each other; what was the reason behind such a strong response from his end?

She sat next to him but didn't dare to speak a word or confront him. But when he did not speak at all for several minutes, she decided to ask him "What happened back there? You do not look okay to me? Would you please tell me Paras?" He almost shouted and answered, "Oh come on Zunaisa! Don't act naïve, he was clearly flirting with you and he was trying to put me down and you on the other hand rather than giving it back to him, kept on lurking and were enjoying his attention and his nonsense remarks." Zunaisa was appalled and couldn't believe what she heard, he straight away assumed things and demeaned her right away in the most ruthless manner. She couldn't come to terms with the fact that he was the same guy she had met or was starting to feel for. He slammed at her and character assassinated her in no time, she felt humiliated and hurt. "I do not wish to dignify your accusations with a response Paras, but I will, however, still say that I wasn't enjoying his attention or anything. I just courteously responded to him and I couldn't curse or abuse him for whatever he said. Your behaviour is totally uncalled for Paras," she got up and left with teary eyes. It was in that moment that Paras realised, he did a blunder, she wasn't aware about the dynamics Siddharth and he shared and it was completely unjustified for him to react the way he did. But he also wondered, was it that he was annoyed at Siddharth or was it that he just got jealous and couldn't control himself seeing another man trying to talk to her let alone compliment her. Either way, he knew that even though Siddharth did what he did because he wanted to take a jab at him, it was difficult for Paras to logic why he reacted the way he did.

He started to regret his behaviour but the damage was done; that following day Zunaisa kept her distance from him and only spoke to him when necessary. He understood that he had to do something to fix the damage caused, he couldn't let her be upset with him. He tried to ask her out for lunch which she vehemently denied. Zunaisa was way too hurt by his unwarranted behaviour but Paras was also determined that he would win her back come what may. Since it was a weekend ahead, everyone got off work earlier than usual. Zunaisa, too without wasting any minute packed her stuff and stormed out and this time she did not even care to inform or report to Paras that she was leaving.

She was standing outside trying to book a cab for home, Paras followed and walked up to her from behind. He held her hand from behind, she turned around, "Why are you here? And why are you holding my hand? Aren't you scared about people looking at you now? I do not wish to be branded with rubbish accusations anymore. You are so ignorant and illogical that you might end up saying I am trying to do things to get your attention too." She stomped away and pulled her hand back. It was obvious that she was hurt, angry and totally mad at him and he knew that he rightfully deserved that reaction from her, however, he wasn't going to give up so easily.

"You are upset and angry, I acknowledge that and I deserve it as well but please Zunaisa, give me a chance to explain myself. Siddharth and I don't get along. He just leaves no stone unturned to provoke me, and seeing you with him, I just don't know why or how I got triggered. But I promise you, Zunaisa, this will be the first and the last time that I behaved with you in this manner. And I do not care who is here and who looks at us, what matters to me is YOU. Please don't leave me like this I... I...I don't want to lose you please," he almost choked and could barely speak and hear himself anymore.

His eyes were moist, Zunaisa was baffled although all his reactions and words did not completely make sense, nonetheless, it did make one thing obvious that there were some emotions from his side too, if not as deep as hers, but there definitely was something. This was the same guy who lashed at her and now was on the verge of breaking down in front of her. She saw him so vulnerable for the first time, and considering that he was this reserved guy, she knew he wouldn't break down or express his vulnerable side so easily in front of anyone; given how empathetic Zunaisa was, she realised that beneath the thick exterior of a man was an innocent soul who wanted to be read and understood, and her heart yearned to help him. She just wanted to make him happy and feel secure and give whatever she has in her capacity to this man.

He was strong, aggressive, dominating yet soft and gentle. There was an unfathomable amount of charm and allure in him which drew her closer to him in an inexplicable way. He was all right and all wrong at the same time and she just couldn't get enough of him. He played with her angel and demons like a stunning magician. Her heart ached and she could no longer see him like that, his words pulled all the right strings and melted her heart.

She held both of his hands firmly and placed her hand on his chest, as if she wanted to ensure that he was alright and felt safe. "Hey! Hey! Hey! Here, look at me, I am here with you. I am not going anywhere. It is alright, you reacted in the heat of the moment and that is fine. It happens. Okay? Just relax," she reassured him and embraced him softly. Her touch was warm, delicate and comforting, the moment she hugged him he felt like melting in her arms; he could catch the light pleasant scent of her hair that lingered around her. It wasn't just her cologne, she naturally had a sweet, soothing and nurturing body scent around her. He wanted to be there for as long as he could and never come back to reality but his alertness got activated and he regained his senses and self.

He couldn't stop smiling and blushing; that brief argument only pulled them way closer than they could have possibly thought of. He turned her towards him, and gazed deeply into her eyes with intense passion and said, "You are one of the most understanding women I have ever met Zunaisa, I am really fortunate to have met you. And your eyes speak more than you do. Allow me to make it up to you and take you for dinner followed by a drive. Would you please join me, Miss Rizvi?" She smiled softly and agreed to accompany him.

Paras decided to treat and surprise her to his favourite spot which was a few hours' drive from the city. The drive was rather more intimate, romantic than ever, they felt closer and more attached. He would nonchalantly entwine his fingers around her and play with them, she would in turn make some drawings on his palm and pretend to read them. They would joke and laugh uncontrollably, and whenever there would come a song, they both liked, they would scream at the top of their lungs and sing it out loud; it was truly an experience for them. It was as if the Cupid was smiling at these lovebirds and was shooting its arrows right at them; and what was more interesting: was that the arrows were seemingly hitting the bullseye; everything around them exuded passion, ardour and love.

After a thoroughly fun filled drive, they arrived at their destination, the place was strikingly large and spread across a wide area. The theme of the resort was an amalgamation of local highway restaurants, the kind that one would find in the suburbs and other rural areas of India, coupled with high-end decors and other amenities to give it a modern twist. The resort was called *"Nagar Dhaba."* Paras would come here all the time and enjoy the food here but to him the biggest selling point of the resort was the nearby lake where he would sit for hours and soak in the view. Zunaisa's eyes were brimming with enthusiasm, it was her first time at this resort and she was impressed with the charm it had. "This place is beautiful, Paras! So sweet of you to bring me to your favourite place. Should we walk around and explore a bit?" She was exuberant and extremely happy to be there with him. Paras decided to order some of his favourite Punjabi-styled stuffed parathas and some buttermilk, which were considered to be North Indian delicacies, and then walked up to the lake with her. He wanted to show her what he liked and enjoyed; it was his way of opening himself to her.

Zunaisa was thrilled and happily agreed to sit with him by the lake. The lakeside area was painted with lush green trees and bushes, a vividly clear sky with traces of some scattered clouds and a gorgeous sunset view which was bursting with the colours of pink, orange and a hint of yellow. The sky and the sun were beautifully reflecting back at the lake offering a breathtaking view. She always thought that she was a mountain person but that day she felt different, she had never really enjoyed or taken an interest in lakes or beaches or even the type restaurant she was trying that day with him; was it that she was enjoying the lake or was it because she was there with Paras which made it feel more special for her? She was definitely curious to know what was happening with her, she was beginning to change a bit and explore the things which she ordinarily would be hesitant but when Paras would be around, she was willing to embrace the change, she wanted to learn and adapt whatever he liked.

From the bottom of her heart, she knew he had won a place in her life; he was more than a friend or mentor. He was all that she ever desired and wanted. She was engrossed and lost in the moment with him, resting her head-on her arms, she continued looking at him lovingly and paying full attention to everything he had to say or talk about. Paras continued to talk about his likes and dislikes, he shared some of his childhood and college stories, he was organically opening up to her. He felt safe around her, her aura was comforting and calming, the kind that he was seeking for all his life.

"I wasn't always this shy and reserved guy, Zunaisa, in fact I was one of the most notorious and happy kids in the town. I was infamous for my pranks and jokes but then back at school I was bullied by this one rich brat if I may say, he knew my family dynamics and he was one of my neighbours. I am not typically close with my family, Zunaisa. My parents don't get along and my sisters never really cared for me that much. And this boy? He gossiped and spread rumours about me and my family and all that he knew. I mean what can a 13-year-old do about all this? I was devastated and just wanted to run away at times," he shrugged and looked down. He recollected himself and continued "I have no idea why I feel this pull around you Zunaisa, I cannot keep my guards up around you. There is something about you and I want you to be there for me, with me always and forever. I may not be perfect but this moment right here with you, sharing it with you feels more than perfect. I want to see many more sunsets with you and begin my mornings looking at your beautiful face and the adorable person behind these eyes," he kissed her hand and gently placed it on his chest.

She scooted a bit closer to him, gently rested her head on his shoulder, and wrapped her hands around him. The interplay between these two very different people with different personalities was beading into a deep bond. They were certainly opposite to each other in many aspects, however, there was one thing in common and it was that they both craved love and intimacy and shared mutual admiration for each other. She was slowly able to understand the true person that Paras really was, there were many layers to him and there were possibly a lot of wounds and unresolved issues. She appreciated the fact that he opened up to her and now that she knew that there was a small little boy inside him who craved love and understanding, she decided to be there for him always and be his support through thick and thin.

Bullying and other childhood traumas often remain unresolved, even after becoming an adult. These issues may affect and alter our decisions later in life. It is generally noted that, if these traumas are not addressed, then some of the victims of such abuses become cynical adults or feel the need to prove themselves beyond perfection to the world because they were bullied and put down in childhood. Thus, when they become adults, they try to compensate for their lost sense of self by either being reserved, completely cold or snooty to everyone around.

These unresolved issues can create havocs and abnormalities in a person's life. Therefore, it is always important to address them in a safe space so that they do not meddle with our personal lives. Almost every second person has some childhood trauma or other allied issues and it is completely normal, and there is absolutely no point in trying to stigmatise it. All these life experiences help in building our unique personalities and each trauma or setback is here to teach us something; we just have to pause and reflect at it. There is absolutely nothing wrong if we don't have an ideal life or family as per the preordained societal norm but what is more important is that what we make out of the hurdles that come across our way, does it make us a better and resilient person? Do we become soft and more compassionate so that next time someone is in a similar situation, we can help them navigate through the predicament, or do we choose to bite our fingers in annoyance and question as to why we were put in this situation or test? No life is all straight line, it comes with curves and the curvier your path the more resilient you shall become. And the first moment of triumph begins when we accept these challenges and try to learn from them rather than questioning it or developing an animosity towards people or life in general. Acceptance is the key.

YOU IN EVERY BREATH

All love stories bloom in their own time, their own pace and there is no right or no wrong when it comes to love. One cannot define love in tangible terms like years or months. There is no concrete map in love, it is unpredictable, uncertain but it does come with an unfathomable emotion unique to every individual, you just have to allow yourselves to feel your feelings. It is possible that you may fall in love when you least expect it, or at times you may fall in love with someone who you never got along with or never thought about, you can also fall in love at any age, any moment.

Sometimes it takes a while for the love to blossom and at other occasions you may fall in love at the first sight, nonetheless, the point remains that love is a feeling that cannot be narrowed down to logical precedents rather it supersedes logic and defies all the odds. Love teaches you about life, it enriches you with lessons; some lessons are made of roses and the others are made of thorns but what is a rose without its thorns and what is love without its storms?

It was starting to get dark, they both decided to head back home as they were a bit far away from the city. They walked to their car and Paras started driving back to the city, this time they decided not to turn on the music, the whole experience in itself was musical and magical. All through the drive, Zunaisa placed her head on his chest while he drove slowly and safely. She took the liberty to touch and feel his chest and tight torso; playing around with her hands and sporadically feeling the cuts and muscles around his forearms. She could hear his heartbeats, which were slow and steady as though he was at peace and so was she. She fluttered her eyes and gently drifted off to sleep, Paras looked at her and smiled. He kissed her on her forehead while she was still curled up in a peaceful sleep holding him and murmured, "I will protect you and never hurt you Zunaisa, and I will make you the happiest. I promise."

He decided to drop her directly to her house as he did not want her to take a cab since it was pretty late. They reach their destination, he tenderly nudges her to wake her up, she looks at him with all the love in her eyes, smiling as though she had so much to say and so little of it that she could speak; she was hoping he would hear the words she left unspoken before him. She whispered in his ears, "This was the best sleep I ever had. Thank you for everything Paras, thank you for what you are and what you did. You opened up to me and that means everything to me," her lips gently brushed his ears while she whispered. Paras felt a sudden jolt of passion and evoked sense of arousal; he knew he wanted her but he was a man of principle, too, he wouldn't cross any boundaries or initiate unless it was mutual. He recollected himself and kissed both her hands instead. "I shall see you soon, Miss Rizvi. In fact, let me plan something and I will get back to you with the details," he said.

"So be it, Mr. Sethi. I shall see you soon! And just by the way, it would be unfair if I don't reciprocate your forehead kiss," she winked at him and planted a generous peck on his cheeks. He was astonished and perplexed while he thought she was in deep sleep, she did hear him talk in intervals. Whatever it might be, he was happy and overjoyed. "You are very smart, Zunaisa. I thought you were in a deep slumber but good for me, I got back my kiss with interest." They both burst into laughter, she got down and walked up to her house. He stood outside to ensure she walked up to the gate safely and followed her for as long as his eyesight could, till she disappeared.

He then drove back to his house, exuberant, content and happy. He was humming a tune of his own, even the honking of cars seemed like melody to his ears. The world feels different when you fall in love: you find beauty in mundane things, you feel full of life, ready to face anything head-on that may come forth. He pulled his car windows down and took out his head trying to grasp in the cold air and screaming with enthusiasm and hooting, the bystanders and cars passing by would either look at him in annoyance or amazement. One of the passersby on a bike screamed and yelled at him and said, "Have you lost your Mind? Or are you blind in love? Can't you see you are on the road? Drive carefully you idiot." The usual Paras would have either not responded at all or would have engaged in a fight with the man but this Paras was a different man now, he screamed and replied, "Yes! Yes Sir! I have lost my mind and heart to her. And I think I am not just blind but in fact I am head over heels for her. Cheers brother, cheers," he hooted and drove past him with speed; he was high not just any high he was high on love. He just couldn't wait to see her again.

She tried to tip-toe and creep in her room without being noticed but one could barely escape the sharp gaze and attentive eyes of her mother. "Care to tell me where have you been all this while? I left you so many calls and texts and you did not bother to respond to any of them? Do you have any idea how worried we all were? You are really behaving odd these days Zunaisa, don't force me to take any harsh steps, take this as a warning from me," her mother reprimanded her.

She knew she was in trouble and lying to her mother was not really an option, she was aware she could read past her lies but she couldn't risk telling her about Paras yet, therefore, she tried to make an excuse about being swamped with work and promised her that she won't repeat this mistake next time and marched back to her room. Her sister overheard the entire conversation from the shared wall of the corridor and waited for Zunaisa to enter their bedroom so she could confront her. All her excitement and smile had melted away and disappeared by now, being sternly warned and admonished by her mother wasn't exactly a pleasant experience after the beautiful day she had but however the spark in her eyes were still intact. She entered her room and saw Shanaya sitting upright in the most confrontational stance ready to plough and pry her about her life. Zunaisa scoffed and said, "Now you too? Are you also going to lecture me like mom did? I just got buried in work, and I have already apologized to Mom for this. So please spare me with your admonition, Shanaya."

Shanaya pulled her to the bed and hushed her down with her hand and said, "Stop with your theatrics right now and listen to me Miss Zunaisa Rizvi, you can lie to the whole world, you can even lie to yourself but you cannot lie to me. I know since you wore diapers, you better not play this hide and seek with me. I can read your eyes and see the shine in them. Now tell me right away what is cooking with you? You are not your usual self lately, you are waking up early, you are coming back late, you are significantly chirpier than usual. You are paying extra attention to yourself. Singing around the house. What is going on? All of this cannot be because of your work. There is definitely something more. Oh wait!!

Don't tell me this has got something to do with that guy you met that night?"

Shanaya's eyes popped out when she connected the dots in her mind, it was all rhetorical as though she answered her own questions. She continued, "So it is him? Gosh, look at you, blushing and fluttering at his mention." Shanaya was right Zunaisa couldn't lie to her, she blushed and nodded. Shanaya gasped in utter shock and excitement, they both giggled and jumped together in circles.

"I mean...What? How? Where? When? How did you meet him again? When were you going to tell me about him and all this? Give me all the details right now!" Both the sisters sat with a tub of ice cream ready to dive into the whole story; Zunaisa narrated to her every detail as to how things advanced and unfolded; from the first meeting at the court, then working together in the same office and all about their date and drives. Shanaya just couldn't believe what she was hearing, she was happy beyond measure, she said, "And he came to drop you here? Today? Oh my Gosh ZEE! Your eyes tell me a lot has happened, don't you dare give me half-hearted details," she tickled and teased her. Both the sisters were pretty comfortable with each other and Zunaisa knew she could share the details about the intimate moments she experienced today with her sister, with no fear of judgment.

Zunaisa replied "Yes Sherlock! You cracked it, I mean yes, we did get a little close, I mean we hugged and we sat together…and…and…" Shanaya gasped and her jaw almost dropped, "And? And what? Did you? Wait, did you two?" Zunaisa quickly responded, "No, no, no…we didn't do anything silly! Come on! I mean I just gave him a peck on the cheek that's it. But there was something more, I felt closer to him emotionally, closer to his heart, closer to who he truly is," she got lost in her own response and zoned out while looking outside her gigantic windows as though she was replaying all the moments in her mind.

Shanaya shook her "Oh, hello, Miss Hopeless Romantic, you are talking like a nomadic lover! Here you are completely lost in him. And what about this Paras guy? Does he feel the same? How can you trust him so much? What if he is a player and he is just pretending? Has he proposed to you or expressed his feelings? You are such a smart girl Zee, don't be so gullible." Shanaya got visibly concerned and alarmed, knowing how soft and emotional Zunaisa was, she was worried about what if this man breaks her heart and trust.

Zunaisa tried to convince her sister although she knew it was going to be difficult to convince anybody to believe or comprehend what was going on between the two of them. What lovers feel can only be experienced, interpreted and understood by them, to the world the lovers tend to be like no less than nomads; but the lovers take pride in being misunderstood by the world for they only wish to be read and understood by their lovers. For them it is the love that makes the world a better place to be in and the rest just ebbs and flows.

Zunaisa gently pacified her and responded, "I understand that you are concerned but trust me Paras is different, he is not like the other guys. You know what? Let me plan something, how about a plan a meeting for all of us? You, Rey and my girls can meet him. Apala, Annie and Monica are coming to Delhi, too so this will be a great hangout. And when you all meet him, I am sure you will like him. He is the best." Shanaya agreed to the proposal but deep down she wasn't entirely convinced, something was bothering her but she hadn't seen Zunaisa this happy in a very long time, therefore, she decided to not let her intrusive thoughts take over and joined her sister in celebrating the joyous moment.

Both the sisters spent the night talking and reminiscing about some childhood stories. Now that Shanaya's wedding was also around the corner, they were both happy and a tad bit sad for they would miss these nights spent together. Nonetheless, they made the most of that moment and chatted all night; while Zunaisa was still talking and didn't hear Shanaya speak for several minutes she turned around and saw that she had fallen asleep while talking. Zunaisa smiled and tucked her inside the blanket and turned off the night lamps and got to her side of the bed and decided to sleep too. She rested on her side and held on to her pillow tightly as if to control her loud thoughts and forced her eyes to shut but it was as though she was fighting an uphill battle in which she failed miserably. The night was silent but her thoughts were loud which were craving and stifling to be heard and echoed, she was missing him and wanted to talk to him; she surrendered to her burning desire and decided to text him; who can possibly wrestle with a heart in love after all? A heart in love is as stubborn as a child, it wants what it wants.

She typed the message and sent it to him *"I have always liked the distant things: the sky, the moon and now? YOU... I wish I could see you now!!! xx."* To her surprise, Paras immediately responded as though he was just sitting there waiting for her to message. The reply read: *"I have been trying to run away from my thoughts, but the truth is you are here in my mind, in my heart and in my soul. And ever since I met you, you never left. Can't wait to see you, Miss Rizvi."* Her cheeks were flushed as she read the message, and her heart started to pound in excitement. She wanted to scream and dance all around, her happiness knew no limits; she couldn't have asked for more. She just couldn't wait for the sun to shine so she could see the apple of her eye, she rolled up herself in her blanket and fell asleep.

"Get up Princess! It's Ten past Nine, you have been curled up still. Get up now or else you will find your mother coming for you next," his father gently brushed her hair and tried to wake her up but it seemed her daughter was enjoying her peaceful sleep and a pleasant dream. "Two minutes Dad! I will just come and join you all, I need to finish this dream I am seeing," she could barely open her eyes and responded to her father half asleep. "It has been a while since I have seen you smile in your dreams! I will let you be my child. I wish you all the happiness of this world has to offer."

Her father kissed her forehead and left for his shoot. He was mostly travelling out of town for work given his work profile but whenever he had the time, he loved spending it with his family. There were days when the children wouldn't see him at all especially when they were in school because of the tight deadlines and graveyard shifts but his father was solely trying to give more time to his family now. Since, Shanaya was also going to get married his father felt more emotional for her daughters, his heart ached but as a man he was also conditioned to some extent to not show real time emotions but he loved his daughters too dearly to succumb to the societal pressure and did not shy away in expressing his love and affection. If the kids had to be admonished, especially the daughters, Aquib would take a step back and let Nikhat take charge, naturally one parent has to be slightly strict to school the children. A healthy balance of love and admonition is paramount for a healthy childhood and a key tone of exemplary parenthood.

Her alarm rang for the tenth time, she finally got up and stretched herself. It was evident that she slept like a baby last night and the first thing she did before anything was to check her phone. The phone notification read: *"One new message from Paras."* She hurriedly opened up and read it.

"Hey Beautiful! I am sure you are still in bed and sleeping peacefully. I wanted to call you and wake you up but then I thought you must be looking so cute right now, God, I can't wait to see you sleep and admire you endlessly. I want you to read this message first thing when you wake up. And by the way, put on your most sporty look. We are going for some games later today. I will pick you up at 1. See you soon."

Her eyes twinkled and sparkled in anticipation, she couldn't wait to meet him; but before anything she had to first diffuse the situation at home since everyone was suspicious of her behaviour, she had to ensure that things remained calm and composed. She decided to quickly freshen up and join everyone at the breakfast table.

She entered the dining room nervously, thinking she possibly hit yet another strike at pissing her mother off. She was all prepared to get the cold treatment from her mother, but to her surprise, she appeared normal, and it looked like everyone was enjoying their usual chit-chat and food. Perhaps it was the slump and harmony sponsored by the weekends, the weekends at home were typically slow mornings and everybody liked to take their own sweet time to do their chores and took their time to unwind.

For now, everyone seemed pretty calm and put together, but she started contemplating how to address her mother or possibly tell her that she had to go out. She had her inhibitions: what if her mother reads through her excuses? She was anyway, hating the fact that she had to time and again lie to her, but she knew that her mother was protective of her, and she may not fully understand the dynamics she shares with Paras.

But then Shanaya rang in her mind; she knew she could back her up and convince her mother, so she gathered her courage and told her mother, "Mom, I want to tell you something. I feel, and I know, that I may have been behaving oddly, but I am not doing anything wrong. I wanted to apologise to you for everything." Nikhat hugged her and said, "You owning and acknowledging your mistake is more than enough, my love. Now, come on kids, get to your rooms, and get ready for the brunch; I have booked us a table at our favourite restaurant."

The moment she heard that her mother had planned a brunch, her heart sank she was supposed to meet Paras later that day; she started fidgeting in anxiety and frantically started to look around contemplating as to how could she come out of this situation, what was she going to tell her mother now? If she didn't go it would upset her mother and she did not want that, the thoughts raced on her mind and made her restless.

Her mother noticed her tensed face and got alarmed, "Are you alright, honey? You are all sweaty and fidgeting. What's the matter? Here, have some water." She tried to calm her down. Zunaisa knew she had to tell her mother about Paras, if not much, but at least that she was planning to go out with him. She hated that she had to pick and choose between Paras and her family. On any given day, she would choose her family and sacrifice her all for them, but she really wanted to spend the day with him, especially after the message he left her, how could she bail out on him?

Zunaisa mustered the courage and told her, "I am fine, Mom. I have been meaning to tell you about this guy. His name is Paras, he is a friend of mine, and my mentor at the office. He is really nice and sweet. I wanted to tell you about him sooner but all of us were occupied with something or the other and I never got the chance to come and speak to you about him. And I am sorry, Mom, but we have already planned our day together. We are going for some games. Please Mom, I really want to go. Could you please excuse me for brunch today? I promise to join you next. Please Mom." She coaxed her mother and her eyes started to well up in persuasion, she wanted Paras more than anything.

Despite the usual healthy admonition that Nikhat channelised on her children, which was indeed for their betterment; she was a very understanding mother overall. She knew her daughter in and out, and the fact that she was a grown-up now, she would naturally develop feelings and nurture new relationships in her life. She wanted to be a friend first and gave her best to be understanding and friendly for all her children. Her aim was that her children should never hesitate in expressing themselves freely in front of her, and if push comes to shove, her children should come to her first, and she would do whatever it takes to help them and lend them her support.

She wanted her children to live freely, of course with reasonable restrictions; otherwise, if you continue to reprimand and deny all the liberties to your child then the fear of repercussions or breaching the protocols becomes redundant and in turn it makes the children rebellious. She wanted to keep a healthy balance of freedom and restrictions.

Shanaya jumped in to save the possible sinking ship, and lent her reassurance to her mother. "Mom, Zee is right. This guy sounds pretty chill from what I know. I think we should let her go with him. She should be fine." Her mother chuckled at the bond that the sisters shared, they would always look out for one another through and through. However, Nikhat was definitely concerned for her daughter but she appreciated her intentions of wanting to steer clear of any unnecessary suspicions that may have created a mayhem and decided to keep her in loop. She looked at Zunaisa and caressed her face and said, "Honey! You don't have to be so worried and anxious, okay? I am happy that you decided to tell me what was behind the curtains after all. It is alright if you would like to go out with Paras. But promise me, you will be alert and share your details with all of us at the family group. We all trust you, my love. However, we still have to take our cautions, alright? Now off you go and stop with your waterfall at once." Everyone burst into laughter and merry and the tensed mood subsided.

Zunaisa couldn't believe what she heard, she hugged her mother tightly and kissed her cheeks, "You are the best Mother in the history of ever, I love you." She quickly winked and blew air kisses to Shanaya as well. Following that, she hastily advanced to her room to get ready to meet the man of her dreams.

"Games and her? Mom why on earth are you even allowing this? I have met this guy and I did not like him. You have to stop her. This guy looks like trouble to me," Rey said, who was visibly upset and angry. Shanaya retorted, "You have barely met him, what are you talking about? This is just your brotherly and manly instincts talking. Just let her be dude, and don't try to bad mouth him now, Mom is chill about it, too. So just shut up, okay? And take it sportingly. He is trying to introduce her to new things. What is the harm?" Before the tension and a full-blown argument could brew, Nikhat intervened and diffused the tension.

"Both of you need to calm down! I have made my decision and there is no need for you both to deliberate on this topic anymore. I will look after this myself. Now my adorable kids, I don't want us to be late for our brunch. Let us all go and get dressed." Soon after, they all left for their respective rooms.

Something in her hinted that this day would be more special than ever, and she should probably do something for Paras to make it extra special for him. "Hmm, I want to do something special for him and his message did say that I should be wearing something sporty, umm so maybe I will ditch my heels and wear my sneakers? I think he would like that and on second thoughts how about I write him a handwritten note? Do men like it? Well, I don't care about all the men, I know my Paras would like it. I will go grab some paper," she started to look around for pen and paper.

Shanaya was standing at a distance and listening to her yap all along to herself and couldn't stop giggling. "My, oh my! Looks like the love bug did bite you, Zee. I will write a letter for my Paras. I will wear sneakers for my Paras. Gosh! I can't stop laughing," she teased Zunaisa.

Zunaisa's face was flushed. She felt embarrassed and annoyed. She knew this was yet another banter of classic Shanaya. She jumped to reply to her in the most confrontational tone she could bring herself to and said, "Eavesdropping is bad manners, Sister! This is really mean of you to overhear and spy on me like that. There is no love bug or love. We are just hanging out and I assumed wearing shoes for the games is more appropriate."

Shanaya laughed and replied, "Like I tell you always, you can lie to the whole world and to yourself but not to me. And now that you are at it, just wear something comfortable. I suggest that you wear that white sweatshirt. It looks really good on you. I am heading for the shower now. Toodles!" She winked at her and hopped into the bathroom.

Zunaisa blushed and smiled, she felt overwhelmed with the kind of support she had from her family; she decided to pick the white sweatshirt her sister suggested and pair it with white sneakers and baggy cargo pants. She took her time to get ready, she had to surprise Paras after all, she made a messy bun and left her usual flicks carelessly lurking around her face. She kept her face clean with only a slight hint of blush on the cheeks and some tint on the lips. She looked fresh and alluring, she sat on her study table and took out a paper and wrote him a letter and to make it extra special and thoughtful she left her lip imprints at the bottom of the letter.

She couldn't contain herself or her excitement and wanted to give him the letter and see his reaction. Soon her phone rang. It was Paras, he was waiting for her outside her house to pick her up. She waved and greeted everyone at home and rushed to the gate to see him.

He was casually leaning on his black Sedan car, holding a huge bunch of pink roses and purple orchids wrapped beautifully in a soft pink paper. He was standing tall and sharp, looking dapper in his beige linen trousers, a black turtle-neck sweater and black suede loafers; his jawline was visible even from a distance and his black aviators added more charm to his already attractive personality.

He was looking around waiting for Zunaisa to come. His wandering eyes finally met hers, he smiled as broadly as he could; his eyes sparkled when he looked at her. He waved to her and could barely control his happiness and excitement when he saw her.

She quickly walked to him and hugged him. He held her tightly and noticed that she had to rise on her toes to reach him, which he found adorable. He noticed that she would fit perfectly in his arms, and it felt as though he could lift her around like a feather. He felt stronger around her, she activated his natural masculine instincts to protect her and he loved that. He loved how calm she made his nervous system feel, the warmth of her skin, the captivating fragrance around her which he relished.

"You look more pretty than I remember. What's the secret of your beauty, Ma'am? Even these flowers cannot match you and your beauty," he gave her the bouquet. Her cheeks turned red, "Well, the secret to my eternal beauty is that I am a witch, Sir! I hunt down men like you to stay beautiful and youthful," they both chuckled and sat in the car.

They drove to the gaming arcade and when they stopped at the signal, it struck Zunaisa that it was the right time to give him the letter that she wrote for him. "Umm! Here, I got this for you. But please just take a sneak peek but don't read it right now," she said. When he saw the letter, his expressions changed a bit, he wasn't an ardent fan of letters or alike, he found them a waste. He preferred gifts or something one could put to use in their everyday lives, but he didn't want to disappoint her, so he reluctantly accepted it.

However, he inquisitively took a quick look at it, he noticed her lip stain at the bottom of the letter which he gently brushed against his thumbs and murmured to himself, "These are the most attractive pair of lips I have ever seen."

She got baffled at his reaction, it seemed that he was talking to himself, she started to profusely overthink that perhaps he didn't like her gesture or if something was wrong. "Hey? Did you not like it? I wanted to give you something thoughtful so I wrote this for you." Paras realized he had zoned out and quickly got back to his senses and said, "No! I love it! I mean, this is so thoughtful of you. I don't generally like letters and rather believe in giving something a person can put to use, but, umm, I really appreciate it and this lip stain here? I will frame it," he smirked and laughed; Zunaisa too, burst into laughter.

However, somewhere down the line, she did feel a faint ache, for his reaction wasn't quite what she had imagined or hoped for. But she pacified and thought to herself, "Maybe Paras is not into letters and old school romance. I think I should do what he likes instead." She was determined to design her next surprise according to his taste and liking. She was certain and resolved to make her next surprise a memorable one for him.

AND THE DANCING IN THE RAIN

They reached the mall and walked hand in hand towards the gaming arcade. The air surrounding them oozed love and vibrance, and everyone passing by could sense it. They were engrossed in the world of their own. Paras enjoyed playing games of all kinds, be it sports or virtual games he had an immense penchant towards it, he wanted Zunaisa to experience his world.

They started their bandwagon with some air hockey, and Paras realized that Zunaisa was fiercely competitive, which he found really attractive; she concentrated fully in the game and gave her best. They started to get a hang of the arcade and quickly gained momentum by trying their hands on bowling where they paired as a team and won outstandingly. They realized they made a great team together. Later on, they advanced to a game console, which was called Pac-man, and Zunaisa aced it meticulously. She went on to beat Paras's score and danced around in extreme joy.

She flipped her hair with an air of confidence and radiated pure happiness, as though she were the unmatched queen, reigning supreme over the arcade. Paras loved watching her like this, he cheered and supported her, and took pride in it rather than feeling bogged down; although he did secretly let her win in almost all the games they played. But he wasn't really focused on winning anyway, to him the real kick was her precious and generous smile and giddiness that would naturally come out for which he could lose a thousand times over.

She pulled him and started to dance and sway around in joy, he, too, without thinking much joined her. He held her by the waist and she wrapped both her hands around his neck, they both passionately looked in each other's eyes which were craving to speak out loud, they both knew they had found their happy place. That moment was a reassurance for Paras, he knew, she was special, very special indeed and he knew he was in love.

He kissed her forehead and said, "Miss Rizvi, since you are clearly the champion, this poor lad here just expects some food as a consolation. Would you do me the honour of feeding this poorly beaten man?" She laughed and agreed. They walked around cozily, browsing various eateries and stalls to grab something to eat and finally sat at a restaurant. They quickly ordered and started to enjoy their sumptuous food. This particular meal felt typically more delicious than it ordinarily would have, perhaps the fact that they both were feeding each other added an extra dosage of flavour to it. The wait staff and other people at the adjacent table smiled looking at their public display of affection and they both didn't shy away from it either.

After having one of the most romantic meals, they decided to walk around the mall and explore a bit before heading back home but while they were walking, Zunaisa noticed that every now and then Paras's phone would ring and the contact's name on the phone was saved as "Niks".

She noticed that he would continuously reject these calls from Niks and his expression would change each time he would get these calls. Zunaisa asked, "Who is this Niks? Why don't you just answer? Maybe it could be something urgent?" But before Zunaisa could get any more inquisitive or suspicious Paras defended himself and responded, "Oh, it's just my neighbour. He is a silly guy and just forces me to plan with him but I don't really want to entertain him." Zunaisa laughed, "Huh! That means, he seems to like your company. You should have tagged him along or maybe next bring him too, okay?" she said innocently without probing much. Paras felt a sense of relief. "Trust me if Niks ever comes between us it will be a nightmare, now enough of this whole Niks business, let's talk about us," he said and brushed off the topic.

Their exploration continued and while they were walking around, Zunaisa suddenly tripped and twisted her ankle. She almost screamed in pain and burst into tears, "Ahh! My ankle, I can't move it." Paras got alarmed and worried. "Zunaisa, are you okay? What happened? Let me see," he tried to calm her down and gently tried to move her ankle but it seemed she was in much pain.

Without a second and much ado, he wiped off her tears and lifted her in his arms; Zunaisa got startled for a second, she forgot how much pain she was in. He was so strong that he lifted her with such ease as though her weight meant nothing. He took her purse and flung it around his shoulders and started to walk. Everybody around started to gawk and notice them, it was a rare sight. Some group of girls giggled and commented, "Yo! You go girl! He is a keeper." She almost felt a bit shy and blushed, seeing how Paras was unfazed and solely concerned about her and her sprain, which melted her heart. She said, "Paras you don't have to do this, I am okay and I can walk."

He replied, "You are okay Miss Rizvi? Really? Why can't you be careful? What if you had fallen and gotten hurt severely. You are very careless, Zunaisa. Now you will have to explore the whole mall like this, even if it takes one hour, two hours, I don't care, I can walk around holding you and I am not putting you down. Get it?" His tone was slightly stern but she knew he was coming from a place of concern; she knew him pretty well by now. He was super protective and possessive of her which she actually liked. She didn't protest any further and rested quietly around his arms while he walked around carrying her.

While they were browsing someone patted on his shoulder, he turned around. There was a fairly tall and lean girl in glasses, casually dressed in a white tank top and faded blue denim, looking at them with amusement and smirking; his whole face went blank when he saw her. He haphazardly put Zunaisa down from his arms; she got surprised with his reaction and noticed the change in his expression. He stood there blank for several minutes, the girl broke the silence in the most sarcastic way, "If it isn't our very charming Paras after all. Walking and carrying around the mall his new girlfriend, is it? I hope I didn't interrupt your date." Before she could speak any further Paras was infuriated and countered her, "What the hell are you doing here, Priya? And how dare you talk like this infront of Zunaisa. She is not my girlfriend and even if she is then this is none of your business. Stay out of this, I am warning you." He yelled at her and without wasting a minute picked Zunaisa up and stormed out of the mall immediately.

He carefully helped Zunaisa sit in the car and started to drive for home, he didn't speak a word and was evidently angry and she hadn't seen him so raged up like this, that too, because of a girl, she was surprised to see such a violent side of him towards a girl. Who was that girl anyway? What triggered him so much? Why was that girl being so sarcastic? Zunaisa was already in pain because of the sprain and now this whole episode was weighing heavily upon her. She didn't wish to hurl any insinuations at him but she had to confront him; the way Paras reacted suggested that there was something between the lines, she held the steering wheel and said, "Pull over the car right now. We need to talk Paras."

Paras was fuming with anger, he had lost his senses and was breathing heavily; he shrugged her hand away but in that second, he realized it wasn't just anybody it was Zunaisa, he quickly gathered himself, questioning as to how he could behave like this with her. At that very instance, he quickly parked his car and before she could speak; he held both her hands and said, "Zunaisa, I am very sorry for whatever happened back there. I know that I promised you that you would never see my violent side but this has nothing to do with you. I had no idea that Priya would come all the way here. I am very sorry, Zunaisa." But her instincts were hinting and signalling that something didn't feel right, this time she was determined to probe further deep, she wasn't going to let this pass away so quickly; she was way too hurt and angry. "You have to tell who this girl is, Paras? She was being way too cynical about us. I am a girl too and I would never walk up to a couple like that and say such things. Oh, but wait, my bad; we aren't a couple, right? What are we anyway? And of course, you don't owe me an explanation neither does my feelings matter here," her eyes became numb and she looked away.

He said, "You are everything for me Zunaisa and why are you taking this in a different tangent, not every relationship has to have a nomenclature. I know, you and I feel the same way for each other and that's what truly matters right? And let's just not focus on Priya, she is my neighbour and she is a bit nosy and has a habit of sucking up to my family all the time. Can we please ignore her?" But Zunaisa wasn't going to let this subside so easily, she was determined for a valid and plausible explanation. The fact that Paras refuted any association he had with her in front of Priya was engulfing her from all sides; she was distressed.

This was the man she was ready to take the plunge for, but why has he scared to own up what they shared? It was evident that there were strong emotions but why was it so cumbersome for him to acknowledge this relationship or even name it. She failed to interpret or find the logic behind his words. She was a traditionalist at heart; she valued relationships and wanted a genuine bond with all the rights reserved. She wanted all of him, she couldn't help but also feel jealous, her guts were signalling her something; it was hinting that there was more to Priya and Paras than just being neighbours.

It was hard to forget how Paras's expressions were changing when he was getting the calls from the number named as Niks, his face had the same expression when he saw Priya. She felt uneasy and wanted answers, Paras knew that this situation was more sensitive than what he may have conjured and he needed to handle it tactfully.

He lifted her sprained ankle and started to gently massage her. "You look more pretty when you are upset, do you know that? Your anger is justified here and I apologise to my lady. My lady is free to impose a heavy penalty that she deems fit but however, the only humble prayer of this poor petitioner who has fallen head over heels for you is to not dismiss my case and give him another chance," he genuinely pleaded. Zunaisa couldn't help but break at his humour and wit, she knew he had a way with his words and humour which she loved but what was more catching here was that Paras for the first time expressed his feelings, her cheeks turned red.

"There is the smile, I was missing. Zunaisa, I want to express all my feelings to you in the best way possible, I want to do something grand for you but till that happens, never doubt me or my feelings for a second, okay? You mean the world to me." This time he didn't hesitate at all and kissed her cheeks and then her forehead. Her faith in him was reinstated and how, a part of her mind definitely had its fair share of doubts but she decided to go with the flow and not to overthink the whole episode much and rather be focused on their blossoming relationship and the even more beautiful days to come; the day ended on a good note, Paras dropped her home and drove back to his house.

Later that day, Paras was consumed by his rage; he couldn't wait to confront Priya head-on about the whole stunt she pulled. His house was looming with the usual melancholy and doleful signs of his mother. He knew his parents must have gotten into yet another fight but he was too engulfed in his rage and situation to go and offer comfort to his mother. He straightaway barged into his room and dialed Priya.

She answered the phone call, "Oh! Hey babe! You finally called. See, I keep telling you that no matter who you date or go out with you will come back to me at the end of the day."

"Oh, just shut up Priya. What the hell were you thinking? Why did you create such a nuisance in front of Zunaisa? I have told you already that I want to focus on my career and have nothing to do with you. Just leave me alone," he retorted in frustration and angst. Priya responded, "So her name is Zunaisa? Hmm, now I know the secret to your happiness off late. Well, you keep forgetting that whether or not you like it, I love you and your family loves me and it was your father's idea that I should come visit you and so I followed you today only to see you goofing around with your new toy."

Paras and Priya had been together since as long as they could remember. Priya was like a daughter for the Sethi family especially after the tragic accident of Priya's parents, Paras's family had been taking care of her since then. She was like a family to them and Paras's father had a soft spot for Priya and wanted them to get hitched soon. Back in school and college days, they both were inseparable, Paras would fantasize of being married to Priya even though he saw his parents struggle with their marriage but he was convinced that his marriage will be filled with love and only love. She was his first love which he wanted to immortalize into a lifelong companionship but nothing is permanent in this life: no love, no relationship, no feeling, no happiness, no sorrow; everything has a set time and as much we want to hold on to things make it last forever, we forget in the due process that we are mortals ourselves; and as mortals our desire for immortality and permanence is the biggest flaw that we hold onto.

As much as he wanted her back then, things and life had changed with their professions being different and him joining litigation his life had changed completely. He wanted to focus on his life and career, he had a bigger vision for himself and somehow, he could no longer resonate with Priya. She was a nice girl, she offered and showered him with love and support, other than Anirudh he would often confide in her and given she knew her family dynamics he felt safe around her and knew that she came from a place of non-judgement. She was pretty much her lover and best friend all in one but over the years the spark had left, he needed something else.

He tried at multiple instances to sever ties with her completely but the pressure from family kept him hooked and tied and even though he may not feel the same for her. Priya was still as madly in love and lunatic for him as she was on the first day they met as kids. Her whole world revolved around him, especially after the loss of her parents. She had taken Paras as her own, someone she truly cared for with all her heart, and if being with him meant walking barefoot on burning coal, she would do so without a moment's hesitation.

But Paras had to prick her bubble and school her, "We are not kids anymore, Priya. You need to stop with your obsession about me and our marriage. It is not happening and I am warning you. Stay away from Zunaisa. She is no toy. She is super important to me and I love her. Dare you mess things between us."

Priya was stunned and furious at the sudden unfolding of confession from Paras, her heart sank; she felt humiliated and betrayed. "You love her? You are such a player, Paras. You think you can be happy with her? Paras, you have tried to move on from me for so long, you tried to date so many women but you kept saying my name and kept coming back to me. I guarantee you, the only us is you and I. You will come back to me and I know it. This so-called love isn't going to last. Goodbye!" She hung up the call.

He felt as though his legs had no strength left to sustain him, he fell down on the floor motionless. Priya's words echoed in his ears, could she be right? What if his feelings are just fleeting emotions? Was he doing injustice to both of them? His chest felt heavy, deep down he knew Priya was right; he felt vulnerable around her and whenever he tried to move on from her, he failed, he always failed. He would crawl back to her faster than he would leave, she was his safe haven.

But he also couldn't deny how he felt around Zunaisa; while Priya had the advantage of being aware of him, his family, his childhood, Zunaisa without knowing much about his traumas read him like a book. She could see past his tough exterior. She was like the beacon of light and sunshine in his life and he never had to truly fully express himself but she would quickly understand his words, his mood; she could interpret his soul and heart effortlessly.

Paras knew Zunaisa wasn't just a random girl. He loved her for real, and he would consciously never hurt her, let alone think about any other woman when she was around. She was too precious for him to lose. He decided to call and check on her. She answered the phone call in a jiffy, as though she was anticipating it.

"Wow! Nobody has answered my call right away. Haha! How is your ankle now, Miss Rizvi?" She responded, "Don't flatter yourself much Sir, I was just going through my social media and you just happen to call. And yes, my ankle is a bit better now. I did take some painkillers which I am afraid will put me to sleep now. I will see you at the office later, okay?" She hung up the call and went off to sleep. That night was rather young for Paras, he kept recalling all the fun and lovely moments he shared with Zunaisa coupled with his heavy contemplation, he resolved to start working on something special for her as a surprise. She deserved all the happiness; he would do anything to bring that charming smile of hers to her face, with that determination, he fell asleep.

As the days passed on, Zunaisa and Paras were getting more and more closer to each other, they were spotted at the court together, they were at the office together, they were going out and hanging out together. When away from each other at their respective homes they would spend hours on calls with each other; it seemed that they both were inseparable. They would talk over the phone all night, barely catching some sleep and come to work with their sleep deprived eyes and as much as this would exhaust them; the thrill and passion that the love gave was unmatched, they wouldn't have it any other way.

Love is such a pure feeling that it has the ability to do wonders beyond comprehension. It instils so much zest in you that you feel that you can conquer the whole world or fight against it as long as you have your lover with you. By now everyone at the office, at their homes, their friends were all aware that they were in love. It didn't matter if they confessed it or not, it was evidently out in the open for everyone to witness it.

It was one of their usual rides back to home from the office but then suddenly they were surrounded with dense clouds and it started to rain torrentially out of nowhere. Zunaisa's eyes widened in excitement, she loved the rain and quickly rolled down the windows and stuck her face out to let the fresh drops of rain fall on her bare skin.

"What are you doing, Zunaisa? You will fall sick. Get inside." Paras tried to pull her back in but she was too lost to care and was living her moment. "Paras, can we please stop here? I really want to get wet in the rain, this is such a gorgeous rain shower. I don't want to miss this. Please, pretty, please?" She gave him the most innocent and pleading look which he could barely push himself to deny. He chuckled and said, "Gosh! Those innocent eyes could easily evade anything! Fine, I will pull over but you just have like five minutes for this. Also, I am only allowing you this because you called me pretty, haha!" Zunaisa without wasting a second got out of the car and started to dance, jump, and swirl around like there is no tomorrow. The traffic on the road was rather scanty given the weather; Zunaisa took the full advantage of the space she had where she could freely move around and enjoy her rain.

Paras while still seated was softly smiling and looking at her dance around and enjoying herself, she was all wet by now. Her white top was gracefully hugging her curves and figure, her wet pants accentuated the elegant contour of her flattering form and figure, and her long-wet hair were twirling and swaying to a rhythm of its own, she looked utterly breathtaking, a vision of pure beauty, charm and sensuality; he just couldn't help and admire her endlessly.

She saw him looking at her, so she rushed to him and pulled him out of his car; Paras despised rain. He was one of those who would rather sit at home and enjoy the rains from his home but Zunaisa was completely opposite to him. She coaxed and pleaded with him to join, he knew any protests to not join her would be redundant and he would never be able to escape the charm of her eyes so he agreed and joined her. They both danced and pretended to do jazz and salsa around, their giggles and laughter could be heard from miles away; that moment was everything fun, passion and romance.

He swirled her around and finally gripped her tight from her waist, his eyes piercing right through her; she felt a chill running down her spine. She couldn't gather herself to look up at him completely, they both knew they craved this far too long. She closed her eyes and tilted her head, he got closer to her, their noses touch against each other and they could feel the warmth of their breath, they both were breathing heavily. He closed his eyes and bent a little lower towards her and held her neck with one hand gently; their lips finally met and brushed against each other softly. Their hearts were racing, they were lost in the moment they had waited since forever. He gently nibbled on to her lips and their tongues entwined and started to play along together. He pulled her closer as to deepen the moment and she reciprocated and surrendered to him. The lovers had been finally united in the most passionate way possible, they both opened their eyes and embraced each other tightly like there is going to be no tomorrow, they felt like they were the two halves that had finally met and now they were one.

Paras gently brushed his thumbs around her lips and said, "You know, I used to wonder when would I be lucky enough to get this close to you. I couldn't have asked for more, Zunaisa." She was too shy to say anything but Paras knew what he had to do to make the moment more memorable. "Let's get back to the car and try to pat you dry. You are shivering." He gently picked her up, they sat in the car and drove around the city holding hands and enjoying each second. He stopped a couple of times either to get her something to eat or something warm to drink, he loved taking care of her and pampering her. She too enjoyed his attention to detail and affection.

The moment had only deepened their bond and intimacy; it entwined them closer, emotionally, mentally and physically. Their passion for each other increased manifold, their chemistry was off the charts, they both equally wanted to savour every inch of each other but also wanted to take things slow and at its pace.

Paras said, "You know, I can read your eyes, I want you too, Zunaisa, in fact I want you more than you can ever fathom but I am in no rush. I am going nowhere, let us unwrap our moments slowly and only when you are fully ready. I would love to wait for you and take things further when you want to." She appreciated his promptness to take charge over the situation before they surrender to the inevitable, it was a weak and intense moment between the two.

She appreciated that Paras wanted the whole of her and unlike many who only crave for physical intimacy and just wished to hook up without caring much about establishing an emotional intimacy; she liked that he was different and grounded and rooted like her. She had various suitors and men from different walks of life who tried to woo and court her, however, nobody ever matched her core values. They all just plainly looked at her as a prized possession, beautiful to look at. But Paras wasn't like them, she was happy to uncover this traditional side of him which they shared in common and it only intensified her feelings for him. She softly smiled and hugged him and soon the day ended and they retired to their homes.

DO I REALLY KNOW YOU AFTER ALL?

"It is quite shocking, I mean Niks following you all the way to the mall and doing all this drama in front of Zunaisa, sounds bizarre. I cannot believe that she created so much nuisance, bro. It must be a tough spot for you. But please, know that I will always stand by your side no matter what. But bro if you really like Zunaisa, then you need to choose one; you have to exclusively end things with Niks. You cannot sail on both the boats, you will either drown or will eventually have to be on one boat only, you cannot have both of them. You have to choose, Paras." Anirudh attempted to explain and advise him. Both the friends were lounging casually at the bean bags overlooking the skyscrapers and well-light buildings around; the rooftop at Paras's house was their favourite spot where they would usually unwind and spend a lot of time together chilling, talking about their lives and much more.

Paras was visibly perplexed and concerned, he knew that Anirudh's premonitions were somewhere correct, Anirudh just wanted the best for him. "My choice is clear buddy and it's Zunaisa. She really makes me happy but you are right I may have some sort of feelings lurking around for Priya, too, and it often bothers me thinking that what if the equation I have with her jeopardizes what I have with Zunaisa. I will take your advice and talk things out with Niks or rather end things with her, our vision is no longer aligned anymore. And just for the fact that Niks and I have been together since childhood and have spent almost our entire lives together doesn't necessarily mean that I have to end up with her. I am aware that if we compare the amount of time I have spent with her it will far exceed what I have spent with Zunaisa. But just because I have spent more time and years with her, am I supposed to carry the burden of making it sustain a lifetime? This is no logic and it is wrong, bro. And when I think of it now, I think Niks was an outlet for me over the years. There is a familiarity and comfort around her because she is aware about my life, my family, my parents. I could be vulnerable around her but feelings can change, right? It is possible to fall in love again and I don't see why I should hold on to her just because I have invested my time and years in this relationship. And on the contrary, Zunaisa tends to understand my silence and I feel like a different man in front of her. She gets me like nobody ever has, not even Niks. I have decided, I will call it quits with Priya before she creates any more drama or things turn haywire."

It was evident that more than giving explanation or answers to Anirudh, Paras was engrossed in a moment of self-reflection. He might have been talking to Anirudh but he was in fact talking to himself, nonetheless, he appreciated this one-on-one conversation with Anirudh, it helped him realise what he truly wanted.

To clear the tense air around the conversation and lighten the mood, Anirudh came up with the idea that they should plan a meeting with Zunaisa, now that he had heard so much about her and his best friend had expressed his feelings clearly it was only fair that he finally gets to meet the lady who had turned his world upside down. Paras liked his idea and decided to plan a meeting together. He wanted to introduce Zunaisa to his circle and make her a part of his tiny world. "Yes! This definitely sounds like a plan; I am sure she will be happy to be on board. Let me plan something out," Paras said. The boys then raised a toast and continued their evening with lots of laughter and conversation.

It had been a while since Zunaisa had last heard from Paras, so she decided to call him. "Hello Mr. Sethi, I hope I am not intruding." Paras was more than happy to receive her call, "I am glad you called; Anirudh and I were talking about you. Oh, and my bad, I haven't told you about him yet, he is my best friend since school and my brother from another mother. I want you to meet him. He is also very excited to see you."

Zunaisa was overwhelmed to know that Paras wanted to introduce her to his best friend. He continued, "And if I may request you for something? Could you please wear something traditional, I would love to see you in an Indian suit," Paras requested. Although Zunaisa had already decided to honour his request, she didn't openly accept it in front of him in order to surprise him. She was more than thrilled to join them for a hangout, she genuinely felt special; seeing that Paras wanted to introduce her to a part of his world and meet his people made her feel seen and wanted. She graciously accepted the invite, thereafter, they ran over some other details about work and life and about their blossoming romance. They could speak for hours and hours and still not get bored of each other.

Zunaisa's house was brimming with happiness, fun, laughter and festivities, the wedding was around the corner and some of the relatives and friends were starting to pour in too, they had arranged for accommodation at a close by hotel for everyone. Shanaya's friends Prakriti, Ritu, Akanksha, Shreya, Urvi and others had already come a month before and each day they would either prepare for their dance and cocktail nights and other functions; it was their best friend's wedding after all. Zuanisa's best friends Apala, Monica and Annie and some of Rey's friends were joining the wedding too. This was going to be one of the first marriages in the family and it was all set to be a big fat Indian wedding.

Nikhat, Shanaya, Prakriti, Ritu, Apala, Annie and Monica were at home discussing the wedding itinerary and chatting about the functions, when they suddenly overhear the dishes crackling and lots of spices being cooked from the kitchen. They all got puzzled as to who could it be in the kitchen, the cooks had already left, Aquib and Rey weren't at home and Zunaisa and the cooking were a combination which was next to impossible.

"What are these noises from the kitchen, Mom? Also, it smells so good. I will go check," Shanaya said. Apala added, "Oh yes whatever it is, it smells delicious, Zee cannot even boil water, I will come with you and check, sister." As they both entered the kitchen, their amazement knew no bounds; they stood there, both surprised and in denial at what they saw. The entire kitchen was taken by storm, there were spices, vegetables, different vessels carelessly lying around and in the middle of this chaos, stood Zunaisa wearing an apron.

She was attentively following the recipe on the video; she was running back and forth to ensure she was following the instructions correctly. "Tell me I am dreaming. Zunaisa? You are cooking? Mom, hurry up here, look at Zunaisa is cooking," Shanaya screamed in excitement. Her mother and others quickly ran towards the kitchen and were equally stunned to see Zunaisa. "My daughter is cooking? I can't believe my eyes. What are you cooking for us my dear?" Her mother was filled with joy and pride. Zunaisa was embarrassed and felt overwhelmed, she hadn't cooked a single meal in her life and here she was cooking one of the toughest dishes. She hesitantly responded, "Umm, I am just trying to cook some Biryani for Paras." The delight, the surprise they all had, was wiped out in a second; they stood their blank and confused, unable to comprehend how different she had become. Changes are good, in fact, they are great but how much of a change is acceptable? And is changing yourself completely for someone even a right thing to do?

Zunaisa attempted to clarify, "Guys, before you take it otherwise, I am cooking for him out of my own volition, he has been a great support and I just want to reciprocate. He loves food so I just wanted to cook for him. Can we please not make a big deal out of it?" Nikhat said, "We are not assuming anything, Zunaisa. If you want to cook for your friend, that's good, at least you are trying something new; save some for us and be careful with the flame," she instructed Zunaisa and gestured to Shanaya and everyone to resume their discussion and to let her be.

However, neither Nikhat nor Shanaya were entirely happy. They got more restless and worried for Zunaisa, however, they tried to maintain their composure and hoped that Paras stays true to her and takes care of her the way she deserves. "Don't worry Aunty, we three will go and speak to her and find out what is up with her,"

Annie consoled Nikhat. It was evident that all of them were having their concerns even though at the face of it everyone was trying to be supportive but the way Zunaisa was changing, adapting and revolving her life around Paras was seemingly concerning.

Zunaisa knew somewhere that her mother and sister were not entirely happy although they were trying to be supportive but their concern and inhibitions were clear. She knew they came from a place of concern. "They haven't met Paras, if only they would have met their doubts would come to rest, I will just figure out something and plan a meeting for them, till then biryani for the win. I hope Paras will love this after all I am adding my secret ingredient of lots of love in this. I will go get ready now." She spoke to herself and hurriedly left to get ready to see Paras.

Annie, Monica and Apala decided to talk to Zunaisa, they entered her room and saw her humming and lost in a world of her own, so much so that she was not even paying attention that her best friends were here for her. Of late, she was growing more and more distant with them. She would seldom make an effort to call them and would speak to them once in a blue moon; her life was all about Paras now and to her nothing else mattered.

Monica said, "Care to tell us where you are off to? We were supposed to go shopping today, remember?"

Zunaisa had lost track of the plans and details, her focus was entirely on Paras. She knew she had messed up here.

"Oh my Gosh! I am so sorry guys, the shopping skipped my mind totally, can we please reschedule or could you guys please go with Shanaya and Mom and everyone else? I will join you guys later? I have to meet Paras and his friend. I cannot miss this. It is really important." Her friends were clearly frustrated and angry at her response, they couldn't believe it was the same Zunaisa who cared so much for everyone, the one who was always up to making plans was now ditching them. Her friends had come all the way to Delhi for her but her eyes and attention was fixated on Paras.

Apala was irked and said, "If you are meeting his friend, then take us too. It is high time that we meet Paras, we have to see who this guy who has turned you so different." Annie added, "Yes, Zee you are getting too invested in this clearly. This man has barely done anything for you, he didn't even care to propose to you. You need to hold your horses; you should not be so blind in love." Zunaisa was appalled to see how everyone was reacting to the whole situation. In her mind she was right and the way everyone was behaving was unjustified and wrong. Zunaisa countered, "You guys haven't even met him, all of you have clearly lost your mind. I am not a kid; I can fend for myself. You all are clearly overreacting. I love him and he loves me, too. If I want to do things for him, what is wrong in that? And how does it matter if I am going an extra mile for him, love cannot and should not be quantified. Just let me be, okay?"

They knew Zunaisa since childhood, it was evident to them that she clearly was way too emotionally invested in Paras and her feelings had deepened to an extent where any logic or advice from anyone would only backfire on them. They decided to not intrude much, but however, they were determined that lest things go south, they will be there for her.

Monica tried to smoothen out the rather hot discussion, "Guys, all of you need to calm down. Zee, you have to meet Paras. It is okay we get it; we will manage the shopping. But you have to promise us that you will take care of yourself and arrange a meeting for us with Paras, we want to meet him too, Cool?" Zunaisa agreed and then everyone left, multiple thoughts started to run across her mind while she was getting ready; so much had transpired, it was all too much take in and grasp. Meeting Paras, falling in love, getting close to him, then the whole situation around Priya, Zunaisa's family and friends and their somewhat passive and negative perceptions about Paras, she was in much contemplation and in a melancholy disposition. But she decided to shrug off these feelings and overthinking; and stay focused in the present moment.

The joy and thought of meeting her love filled her with joy and then nothing else mattered anymore. As requested by Paras, she decided to wear a traditional Indian salwaar kameez. She picked up an olive-green suit for the day, she danced and sang around the room, investing her good time in looking her best for Paras. She loved when Paras played with her hair so she let her hair loose and combed them smoothly which went below her waistline; she wore a deep brown lip shade to create a contrast with her outfit.

After getting dressed she packed the Biryani and left for the coffee shop where they were meeting. She was convinced that although everyone at home may not fully comprehend her feelings, she knew Paras would appreciate her efforts and she could no longer wait for his reaction.

Paras and Anirudh were nicely seated and were lounging at the couches of the coffee shop. "Bro, I love this place but now I have a feeling that what if I am the third wheel here? What if Zunaisa and I don't get along? What if I don't like her? I mean you clearly love her; it is understandable but you have to cut me some slack here if I don't like her and don't engage much with her," Anirudh said. Nonetheless, Paras reassured him that he would definitely like Zunaisa and they continued their chat.

The coffee shop was an artsy, warm and cosy place, the décor was minimalistic and rustic with a lot of high chairs and couches and indoor plants sporadically kept around adding freshness and an element of greenery to the space. The place was surrounded with the aromatic smell of coffee beans and other bakery products. The boys were enjoying their drinks and goofing around, but even in that dense aroma of coffee around Paras suddenly noticed a familiar fragrance softly lingering behind him, stirring memories and passion so unmistakable that his heart almost skipped a beat, he didn't really have to confirm who could it be rather even without looking back, he was most certain it was her.

He stood up and turned around, he was awestruck when he looked at Zunaisa, she was donning a beautiful traditional salwar kameez as per his request and was looking truly ravishing and captivating in every sense. In that moment he realised that he was in love with her all over again, he walked to her and politely escorted her to their table. Anirudh was quietly observing all of this and was taken aback to see his friend so transformed, effortlessly chivalrous in her presence. He never saw Paras being so thoughtful for Priya. But Zunaisa had a different impact: a positive impact on him, and it was here for him to see.

They all sat and Paras introduced her to Anirudh, Zunaisa in no time brilliantly engaged with Anirudh and built a rapport with him. Zunaisa was a natural, and her honesty and modesty made her supremely likeable, she would effortlessly speak to everyone be it an older man or a kid, she knew how to ensure that everyone feels seen and heard in her presence which set her apart. Anirudh, who was doubtful about her, couldn't stop gushing over her now; it seemed as if they immediately became great friends. Paras was happy to see them vibe and mingling.

"Feels like, I am the third wheel here, now excuse me for a moment you two, I need to use the restroom," Paras chuckled and left. However, they were having too much fun talking to care much. Paras had mistakenly left his phone at the table and just then it rang, it was a call from Niks; as soon as Anirudh saw the name flash on the phone, his laughing got restricted to a frown and utter shock. Zunaisa immediately recognised the name and couldn't help but notice the change in Anirudh's expression and face. The phone kept ringing a couple of times and Anirudh picked it up and hit his phone on flight mode. In no time, Anirudh's phone began to ring, too.

When Zunaisa saw the same contact name "Niks" on Anirudh's phone, her suspicions rose alarmingly, seeing all of this and her mind started to spin in confusion and anger. Who was this Niks? How come the same name and number was calling Anirudh immediately after calling Paras? Why did Anirudh get so unsettled seeing the call?

She could take no more and confronted Anirudh, "Who is this Niks? I keep seeing this number calling Paras all the time and now you? Paras told me that Niks is a neighbour but why is the neighbour calling you? Why do you all get so unsettled when you see this number? What is the matter?" She was clearly annoyed and wanted answers. Before, Anirudh could clarify or answer; Paras joined them and noticed the tension between them.

"What happened? I leave you guys laughing and now you are both sitting as if something serious happened," Paras said. Zunaisa answered in a rather annoyed voice, "It seems like Niks is very concerned and has been endlessly calling you and Anirudh." Paras began to profusely sweat and started to fidget in anxiety, how was he going to tackle this situation now? What explanation could he give for Niks calling Anirudh? He knew he couldn't evade this confrontation but still he attempted to get away with it with some lame excuse and changed the topic. Anirudh helped him steer clear of the topic and resume the conversation with Zunaisa in order to deflect the mess that was created. Even though Zunaisa didn't react strongly at that moment, she knew she had to do something about it. The meeting that started on such a joyful note, ended with looming tension and utter havoc.

Paras knew it was going to be a tense ride home; he mentally prepared himself for interrogation and confrontation. He knew that Zunaisa would not excuse him this time. Anirudh decided to let them be and sort things out and took a cab home.

He tried to nudge her but she was fuming with rage and brushed his hands away. It was the first time he was seeing her eyes full of anger. "Are you not going to talk to me at all, Zunaisa? You are really overreacting. Why are you making such a big deal out of this? I told you Niks is a neighbour and happens to know Anirudh too, she must have called for some work. She knew I was going out with Anirudh. Now please, stop being so immature and behaving like a kid, Zunaisa. Act like a grown up and stop this nonsense at once."

Zunaisa couldn't believe what she heard, rather than giving an explanation he was calling her immature, pawning the blame to her for overreacting. He was derailing the entire topic and shifting the onus, she could take no more and lashed at him for the first time, "You think, I am an idiot? Yes, you are right, I may be a kid and younger to you but I am not blind. I have seen the look on your face when this Niks calls you. You tell me she is a neighbour? Well, guess what, I am not buying it this time, Paras. Either you tell me what is going on or it's over between us." Paras tried to calm her down but she wasn't prepared to listen.

Soon they got into a verbal spat and things quickly escalated to being ugly. They started screaming and yelling at each other, Zunaisa knew Paras was wrong and was hiding something but he wasn't coming clean and through. Paras on the other hand knew he was wrong and did realise that he should have told Zunaisa about his dynamics with Niks, but he knew that she was too sensitive, and would never fully understand it. In his head, he was right by keeping things hidden from Zunaisa but owning up to his mistake now and telling her his share of the story was something he wasn't ready to do. He stayed on his stance that there was nothing between Niks and him and they were just neighbours.

While their bickering and heckling continued, they suddenly noticed that the car engine had started to make some weird noise, and it finally broke down. "Damn it! Look what you did. The car! Now can you please shut up and let me check? Damn! Could this day get any worse?" He banged the steering wheel and stormed out of the car to check the engine.

The whole situation had taken a toll on her. It was too much for her, she broke down and started to cry but Paras barely paid attention to her and went ahead to look for someone to help either tow the car or get it repaired. To her it felt as though her whole life came crashing down, this was the man she was ready to put everything at stake for and suddenly her feelings and tears didn't matter to him at all. She couldn't help relate all this to Niks.

"This is all because of that girl, I don't even know who she is and why is he so invested in her. She can't be a friend." She continued crying, but just in that instance, she noticed Paras's phone was still in the car, and since he was using Google Maps to navigate, his phone was unlocked. Without a second thought, she picked it up and began to search through his cell phone for all the details about Niks.

What she saw on the phone blew her mind and tore her heart to pieces. She couldn't believe what she was seeing. She skimmed through their chats and photos. They were all so intimate and private; she wanted all of this to be a bad dream that she was seeing.

THE WHITE LIES

Her heart sank and at what she saw and read; she saw a lot of recent messages were about her. Some of them read: *"I see, you are all after her. But this stupid little romance will not last long Paras, you will get bored of her eventually." "You and I are meant to be, you and I will be married." "What do you see in Zunaisa anyway? Looks are all that she has and if you want her looks, fine date her, go around with her but why do you have to ignore me. We can still be together."* She felt sick in her stomach, she could feel a literal tightness in her chest after reading it, she also saw some really intimate photos of them together. She was shocked to see how being a girl Priya still spoke so recklessly about her; all of this was unbelievable for her.

"He has been dating her? I cannot believe that this Niks is none other than Priya, the one that we met the other day. Why has he been lying to me about her? She is not just a neighbour; in fact, it looks like they have been together for a very long time. How can Paras do this to me? I mean it is obvious that they still talk and I don't even know if he is still dating her. Why Paras? Why me?

I have given you my all. Where did I go wrong? Is this true you just want me as a crowning achievement? You have never been genuinely in love with me? How could you be faking all this? I don't believe this. I don't. All this is a lie. I have loved you with all my heart. Tell me what more can I do so that you don't ever go back to her or any other girl." She started to cry uncontrollably, she could barely speak and hold herself together. She distantly saw Paras coming back to the car with someone, possibly a mechanic.

She had to confront him; she got down from the car. It was a bolt from the blue when Paras reached the car and saw his phone in Zunaisa's hand; in that fraction of second he was certain she ran through his phone and must have seen everything about Niks, but he was too shrewd to own up his mistake.

"How dare you intrude on my privacy like that Zunaisa? Have you lost your mind? I have been dealing with your nonsense all day. Enough is enough," he yelled at her. The mechanic stood at a distant overhearing the fight. Although she could barely speak, she lashed at him and responded, "Nonsense? You are such a shameless man, Paras. You are practically double dating the both of us. I feel sick to my stomach. Why didn't you tell me about her? You are so sick. You have sisters too. Why would you fool around me if you were to marry her? Tell me?" she shouted.

He gripped her tightly and twisted her arms behind her. "Shut the hell up, Zunaisa! How dare you call me names and drag my sisters into this? Shut the hell up and mind your business, Zunaisa! You are nobody to question me like this," he yelled back at her. Seeing him getting physically and verbally violent, Zunaisa lost it completely, she pushed and slapped him in retaliation. Never in her life did she ever hit a soul but Paras, the man she was hopelessly in love pushed her beyond the limits.

Paras was seething with rage and couldn't hold back the insult of being slapped by a woman, the man who grew up watching his father as the only dominant figure was conditioned to treat women as a weaker vessel; how could he ever let a woman slap him even if he loved her. In that instant, his anger was beyond comprehension, without a moment's pause; he slapped her back so hard that she fell to the ground.

She was left in shock seeing Paras's retaliation. She could no longer breathe and everything around her began to feel dizzy and heavy. She knew she was having a panic attack but she felt so helpless and numb to do anything, the phone dropped from her hand and she fainted.

When he saw her collapse, he realised the gravity of the mistake he made; he panicked when he looked at her. He quickly got inside the car to fetch some water, he sprinkled some drops on her face and tried to wake her up, he knew that he messed things way bad but at the moment the priority was to bring her back to consciousness; after several minutes she gained back her senses. She slowly opened her eyes and looked at Paras, her head felt heavy and her vision was still blurry. She wanted to say a lot of things, she wanted to scream, yell, ask him questions but she decided not to.

Paras got worried for her, seeing her in that condition his anger subsided, and he tried to calm her down. He knew that it ought to be his loud behaviour that must have taken a toll on her, since she wasn't used to it. He picked her up and hugged her. "Babe! I am so sorry. I am sorry. I just don't know. I have a bad temper and I lost control and slapped you. Trust me, I will never do anything to hurt you, consciously. Let us just forget all this and start afresh, okay? The guy is here, he will fix the car and let us get you home. Okay my love?" She didn't protest or said a word but just nodded and sat back in the car. Even though she knew all the white lies by now, she decided that it was in the interest of both them, that she never confronts him about this ever again and forget all of this like it never happened; perhaps in her mind this was the only recourse she had if she wanted to save her relationship and love. The love that she had was now coupled with a feeling of challenge, she felt as though she is in a race with Priya, and the end goal is to win Paras at any cost. She was willing to take this plunge and despite whatever happened, whatever she saw, she decided to brush everything under the carpet as though nothing ever happened. A faint voice in her head kept warning her but she was too blinded in love to pay heed to it.

Disrespect in a relationship is a glaring red flag and violence whether physical or emotional is unacceptable and should never be ignored or left unaddressed; even though you may love the person with all your heart and you may be ready to give your life but one should never normalise disrespect, physical or verbal abuse in any relationship.

But strange is the quiddity of lovers, they tend to forgo and overlook everything for the sake of their love. They go to the extent of compromising their own self-respect or breach their boundaries for their love, such is the state of a heart hopelessly and madly in love. They say everything is fair in love and war but is it really fair to be at war with yourself, your self-esteem and self-respect for the love?

She somehow started to justify Paras and his actions; her heart wasn't ready to accept that he was wrong even after what she saw; her mind screamed to differ but she hushed it away. She spoke to herself "Paras, loves me way too much to ever hurt me or cheat on me. And it looks like Priya anyway seems more interested in him, but I won't let her take my Paras away from me. I will love Paras more than anybody ever has, I will win him over and love him with every ounce of blood and love that I have in me so that I never have to look for love anywhere else. He is mine." Tears rolled down her cheeks, but she pacified herself thinking that in this moment she was with Paras and that is what she wanted and mattered to her. Even though her mind and gut kept telling her that she was making a grave mistake, but a heart in love knows no logic and the flaws of their lover seems flawless to them.

The mechanic did his job and left, now that his car was retrieved, he felt a wave of relief. She recalled that she had cooked for him and with all this happening she had forgotten to give it to him. She gathered herself and said, "I made some biryani for you. I know you love food. I wanted to give this to you." His heart softened at her gesture. She was a really nice girl, even after what he had done, she was still considerate and he knew had somehow met a gem of a person. He looked at her intensely and compassionately, "I sometimes feel, I don't deserve you or your love Zunaisa. You are too good to be true." He advanced closer to her, and cradled her face and hair, he then kissed her tears away and then her eyes. "I promise this will be the last time that I ever made you cry." His touch gave her chills down the spine, she couldn't help but melt in his arms.

His fingers caressed and traced her neck, she could feel his cold hands and his touch which was tender yet insistent, he came closer and their lips met softly first, then deepened into a passionate one. Each moment broke a barrier between them, the embrace of the lips was like a dance of intense longing and connection. He glided his hands smoothly around the silhouette of her curvy waist, drawing her closer to him and she surrendered herself completely to him. The world around them faded as they lost themselves in the warmth of each other, it felt like that moment suspended in time where nothing else mattered except the shared sweetness of their intense intimacy. Perhaps the fight brought them closer than ever or did it pave the way to something unpredictable, they were too lost in each other to care.

Zunaisa walked into her house which was full of guests and friends, lounging around at the coffee table having a gala time. She had too much going on to join them all right away, and even if she did join them, she knew her friends and family in no time would notice the hollow of her eyes. She walked her way straightaway to her room. She collapsed on the bedroom floor and tears spilt forth like a sudden storm, she was too overwhelmed and consumed by the chaotic cacophony of emotions swirling within her. She felt as if she could no longer differentiate between right or wrong.

Apala followed her to the room and got shocked by her state. "Zee! Zee? What happened? Look at you? I saw you coming straight to the room, Gosh! I am getting worried now. Will you speak up?" Apala hugged her, tried to rub her hands and shoulders but it felt as though Zunaisa had no words to articulate what was going inside her, she kept weeping profusely. She finally found the words to bridge her silence and told Apala everything that had happened. Apala was stunned to find what all had transpired, she couldn't believe her friend was going through so much, she hugged her tightly.

"Zee! My baby! I am so sorry for what happened to you. I mean what is wrong with Paras? How can he hit you back? It looks like he is cheating on you, Zee. We all love you a lot, see everyone keeps warning you; you have to get rid of this guy, Zee. You cannot change or fix him. No amount of love that you give will change him. You are such a selfless person you will keep giving and he won't ever return it to you." Apala couldn't see how Zunaisa was losing herself for him, she tried her best to talk her out of the situation. She tried to explain to her that there was nothing wrong with Zunaisa or her love but she was willingly investing it in the wrong guy; but it was a lost cause now.

Zunaisa was determined to change her fate and give Paras all that she has, "I am not going to quit, Apala. I don't expect anybody to understand me or my feelings. This is my battle, let me fight it. I know I can fix this. Paras loves me and I know he is short-tempered but when you are in love, you have to make sacrifices. And I never expect anyone to return the love or affection I give them. That's not who I am. And I love Paras, I cannot leave him. But you please promise me, you will keep this to yourself. I cannot risk letting everyone know about this.

Please, Apala," she pleaded. Zunaisa then implored her to make an excuse for her so that she doesn't have to go out in front of everyone in that disturbed state of mind and she needed to sleep on it. Even though Apala hated what Paras did to her and wanted to avenge him but Zunaisa and her happiness was way more important to her, with a heavy heart she agreed to be on board with her request.

She then gave Zunaisa some time to herself and joined back others at the coffee table before anybody at home could became suspicious. She lay on her bed, thinking and playing all the moments on loop again and again until sleep finally enveloped her.

The following day, she woke up with a heavy head; all the crying had literally drained her. Her eyes were all puffed up and swollen, she had no energy to get out of the bed and head to the office. It was the first time ever, she felt so distressed that she didn't feel the urge to go to her work, something which she was so passionate about. She picked up her phone and noticed that there were no notifications from Paras, she sighed but she had made a promise to herself that she will fight this over.

So, she left him a good morning text and forced herself out of bed. She barely had any appetite but not eating would have caused ruckus and a lot of speculation which she couldn't afford to tackle. She reluctantly joined everyone for breakfast and prepared herself mentally to be interrogated but she noticed only Shanaya was at the dining table.

"Wow! Look at your face. How is your headache now? Apala told us that you had a really bad one last night, you missed all the fun and games," Shanaya said. Everyone had spent the whole night chatting and playing games. Indian weddings typically are celebrated with a lot of fun and galore and they are no less than any festival and a gala. Zunaisa felt a sense of relief knowing that Apala had handled the whole situation diligently. "Umm, yes, I am fine. I will go get ready for work. I am planning to make something for lunch and take it to the office," Zunaisa said.

It was pretty obvious to Shanaya that she was cooking it for Paras but she decided not to pry much into it and wished her for a day ahead. Although she had no enthusiasm or zest to get ready, which she usually enjoyed the most, she pushed herself to do it anyway and then packed the lunch for Paras. She wanted to surprise him, she reached office before time and waited for Paras to come, only to be informed by the office clerk that he was assisting and briefing the senior for an urgent matter and would be back in office by lunchtime. She got back to her desk and tried to concentrate on her work while still checking her watch every now and then for lunchtime to come soon.

Finally, Paras reached the office and saw Zunaisa anxiously waiting for him, he walked up to her. "Looks like someone has been waiting for me all day, how are you today? You look a bit tired." Zunaisa smiled and nodded, "Yes, I got here at eight because I couldn't wait to see you. And chill, I am fine, I just didn't sleep well that's it. Here, I cooked lunch for you." Her gesture did not go unnoticed by him and his gratitude reflected in his eyes, she felt accomplished; then they sat and ate together.

Days continued, with Zunaisa trying to do new things for Paras each day, from cooking him lunches, to writing him notes, getting him the best of gifts ranging from limited edition watches and clothes. She even went ahead to change her dressing style for him and started to wear more traditional attire because he liked them. Wherever they would go out for food or dates, she would jump to clear the bills. She truly left no stone unturned in pampering and showering him with love. She topped all of this along with her visible physical affection, attention, loyalty and love. It was clear by now that she was more invested in him than he was, Zunaisa's whole world started to revolve around him and for all that she was doing she was expecting nothing in return, she found her happiness in making Paras happy.

"Paras! It's a weekend today and I want you to come with me somewhere. I have something for you," she said. Paras was thoroughly enjoying the gestures and affection; he was being showered with day and night; by now he was laid back in the relationship knowing she was all in for him. "Sure babe, I will come. Just send the details."

He reached the location and was stunned to see the grand set up. It was a large lawn, decorated with orchids and carnations, and some warm lights dangling around. There was a lavish spread across the adjacent table which had a variety of cuisines and munchies to binge on and a large screen with a projector and comfortable couches neatly placed in front of the screen. He hadn't seen such a larger-than-life gesture in his entire life. He couldn't believe that Zunaisa single-handedly had arranged all of this for him. He was thrilled and kept hugging and thanking her for this wonderful surprise. She was happy and content that she outdid herself with this and Paras' reaction to it was priceless; she couldn't have asked for more.

They enjoyed a lovely evening and spent it watching movies, listening to songs on the big screen, eating and dancing around engrossed in a world of their own. They knew they were not just living the moment; they were making memories. Their date ended on a pleasant note.

A couple of days later, it occurred to Zunaisa that it had been a while since her friends and siblings had requested that they wanted to meet Paras. She thought for a change it might be a good idea. So, she finally decided to arrange a hangout for them, although she was very nervous knowing that nobody really liked Paras that much, and he too was a bit reserved and introvert. How would they all get along? Even though her friends and Shanaya readily agreed to the meeting, she knew the real daunting task was to convince Paras for the same.

She decided to call and convince him, after a lot of coaxing he finally agreed to the meeting. "Fine, I will come but know that I am only doing this for you. Also, please don't expect me to talk a lot or do things out of the way, you know that is not my style," he said. She agreed to all his terms and conditions for as long as he was agreeing to meet, she knew she could handle the rest. "Don't worry babe! You be yourself; I will handle the rest. We will see you at 7," she planted a kiss over the call and hung up. They all got ready and reached the restaurant *"Pandora"* which was one of the favourite places of Paras. "Okay, so first this man had no courtesy to come pick us up and now we are here because it's his favourite place? Seriously Zee?" Monica rolled her eyes at Zunaisa.

"Please guys, he is anyway very nervous and introverted, I just booked us a table here so that he feels a bit comfortable. Please don't be so harsh on him and cut him some slack," Zunaisa pleaded everyone. The only choice they had was to cater to her requests; they entered the restaurant and saw Paras sitting upright across the table. He noticed them from a distance, however, consciously remained seated. The meeting which had barely commenced had already started to take a toll on him, he had no interest in meeting them whatsoever, however, he just agreed for the same because of Zunaisa.

They all walked to him. Zunaisa introduced everyone to Paras, he reluctantly exchanged pleasantries in a way that projected as though he was forced to be there which was hard not to notice or even scoff at. Zunaisa could clearly sense the tension and strain in the air and tried her best to ensure everybody felt comfortable. But it felt as though she hit a wall and no amount of effort from her end seemed to bridge the gap.

"Umm, how about I get everyone some mocktails? It's self-service here so, tell me your orders. I will go get them. Cool?" Zunaisa asked. They all gave her their orders, including Paras, she happily took them and went to place them. Monica whispered to Annie, "So, he is just going to sit here like a King while she goes there alone and gets the order? This man is trouble, I am telling you. No courtesy at all." Annie nodded in unison. Apala couldn't help but overhear, "Guys, stop talking when he is right here; we all are here for Zee and let's just stick to this and not talk. Please?" Apala admonished them gently.

While Zunaisa was away, Shanaya and Annie tried multiple ways to strike an engaging conversation with him but his cold stance and dry responses started to bug everyone off. When Zunaisa came back and noticed that things were getting no better, she decided to quickly wind up the meeting before things could turn topsy-turvy. She cleared the cheque and they all left the restaurant.

On the way back home, Shanaya, Annie, Monica and Apala were agitated beyond words, they just couldn't stop talking about how rudely Paras behaved and how off his behaviour was; they were highly disappointed in him. "What was with that attitude? We went there exclusively to meet him and he was behaving as if he was doing us a favour by coming." Shanaya's words were filled with anger and rage. "I agree, I mean, Zee was doing everything. Placing orders, getting the cheques. This guy is not normal. I am an introvert too, but that doesn't give anybody a gate pass to act so distant and rude," Annie added.

They kept discussing and venerating their anger and frustration. Zunaisa was at a loss of words, she didn't really know how to defend him or make the best of the situation. "Guys, I told you he is a reserved type of a guy. It's my fault, he wasn't comfortable but agreed to come for me. And he does things for me all the time and if I wanted to pamper him and all of you by treating you all because I was the host. Why is that such a big deal? Can we not talk about this now, please?" Zunaisa responded. Apala, who had been quite all this while and was aware about everything that had been happening behind the scenes, couldn't take it anymore.

"Oh, just shut up, Zee! This is enough. This guy has crossed all the lines, he doesn't deserve you. He was so disrespectful to us and to you. He doesn't respect or love you either," Apala lashed at Zunaisa. Everyone was shocked at the sudden outburst of Apala, even though everyone was definitely upset with Paras and his behaviour, Apala's extreme agitation got everybody slightly perplexed but nobody pointed it out. Shanaya sensed that the situation was a bit tense therefore; to lighten the mood she decided to take everybody shopping. The group, including Zunaisa, thought it was a great idea, so they all agreed and spent the rest of the day shopping together.

I LOVE YOU!

He sat quietly in his room with the loudest thoughts, recalling each and every moment they had spent together. It had been a roller coaster ride for him, he knew he loved Zunaisa but he wasn't able to understand why it was so difficult for him to let go off Priya completely. He introspected his behaviour, he had noticed that Zunaisa was investing more of herself in him while his efforts were somehow decreasing; he wasn't sure if he was doing it consciously. This was the girl who made him so happy and here, he was being completely complacent to her and her feelings; a sense of guilt and remorse kicked in and he lay flat on his bed realising his mistake.

He murmured, "I should do something for her, it has been a while and especially after a horrible meeting with her so-called friends, I guess she deserves a surprise from my end. Although I have a hunch, her friends must have trash talked about me so much. Ah! Come on! I know her. She won't side with them. Let me do something for her now, and I will make it so grand this time that she will remember it for a lifetime." With that determination, he surfed the internet looking for some creative ideas and spots in order to plan his next big surprise for her.

"Your phone has been ringing continuously, Zee. Who is calling you this early, I mean it's four o'clock in the morning. Just answer the damn phone dude, ughh." Shanaya who was almost half asleep herself nudged Zunaisa. Zunaisa could barely open her eyes herself but when she saw the name *"Paras"* flashing on her phone, she nearly jumped out of bed and hurriedly answered.

"Good morning beautiful and where has Miss Rizvi been? I have been calling you for so long now." Paras sounded doting and very cheerful over the phone call. Zunaisa was surprised and amused at the call and seeing Paras talk like that refreshed her initial days when they first started dating, she liked that he was possibly trying to make amends. He continued, "I have a small surprise for you today and I need your whole day for this, alright? So, no excuses about the wedding and chores. I will come pick you in an hour, okay?" He also requested that she wear something fancy and flowy. Zunaisa couldn't believe what she was hearing; it felt as if her old Paras was back. Even though she was willingly giving all her efforts to him, she couldn't deny how much she had missed this side of him. She was happy and overjoyed with the idea, she quickly agreed and got all set to meet him for the surprise.

She begged and pleaded with Shanaya to be her alibi and to manage things at home so she could quickly leave. Shanaya hesitantly agreed. She hugged Shanaya tightly, "You are the best sister ever, tell them I am off her court or anything, just improvise, okay? I love you. You are the best." She hastily made her way to freshen up and get ready and now that Paras had asked her to dress up for the surprise, she decided to go all in for it.

He waited downstairs for her; she walked out of the gate and when he saw her, he was spellbound. She was elegantly dressed in a chocolate brown maxi dress which clung gracefully and artfully around her body and exquisitely highlighted her flattering curves and figure. He looked at her with the same passion and desire when he first met her. She was indeed one of the most gorgeous women he had ever seen or met, he felt proud and accomplished. Zunaisa, was equally smitten when she saw him all dressed up in a tuxedo, she had never seen him in one, although she was a bit perplexed to see him wearing it, she was too smothered by his charm to think about anything else.

He walked up to her and gently escorted her to the car. Zunaisa noticed his twinkling eyes, they had the same gleam and intensity when they first met; she was elated beyond words. When she sat in the car, she noticed that the back of the car was filled with red roses all over the backseat. A wave of excitement and happiness brushed her, it all felt too good to be true; she pinched herself barely able to curtail her astonishment.

"I know you love roses and trust me the way you look right now you deserve a whole garden, these are nothing in front of you," he kissed her cheeks. Zunaisa blushed and hugged him, "Wow! Paras! These are gorgeous, I mean this is the best surprise ever." He replied, "The surprise hasn't even started yet, my love." He kissed her hand and started to drive to their destination. After an hour's drive or so, they finally reached their destination.

The place looked like a resort and had a lot of open spaces and greenery; Zunaisa was still confused as to what the surprise really was, so she looked around the place trying to look for cues. "Gosh! You little Miss Anxious. Here, I need to blindfold you for this surprise. So, bear with me, okay?" He blindfolded her. The anticipation was now killing her. What was the surprise anyway?

"Paras, I am scared now. What are you doing, I can't even see." "Sssh! Just keep following my lead," he said. A few minutes of walking and they finally stop, he opens her blindfold. She gasped; she couldn't believe her eyes, "A hot air balloon? What? How did you arrange this? I cannot believe my eyes. Gosh! This is the best day ever," she sprang into his arms with all excitement and fervour. "The surprise is still not over, my lady. Now come, let's hop into this thing and I shall talk to you through the sky," he winked and laughed. They both harnessed carefully and got on the hot air balloon, it was truly a great day for them.

Zunaisa felt like she was on cloud nine, he organised and planned such a huge surprise for her when she had no idea or expectation. The view from the top looked breathtaking, it was close to sunrise. The sun came out from behind the clouds and the first few rays caressed their faces, the curling morning breeze added another touch to the whole experience. They both were enjoying every bit of it.

"Paras, this is beautiful. I never imagined or expected something like this. You are the best. But, wait, what is this weird thread thing you tied on my finger?" Before she could realise, a ring slipped through the thread and she saw Paras on his knees. She was surprised and her jaws nearly dropped at whatever was happening, she couldn't believe any of it. Paras slipped that ring in her ring finger and kissed her hand and said, "I have been meaning to say this to you since the first time I met you. You are the best thing that has ever happened to me Zunaisa. You deserve all the happiness. I love you!" She was speechless, not knowing what to say, how to react, she didn't expect any of this, if she ever did think of it then it was only in her dreams or imagination.

And here she was, living her fantasy with the love of her life; someone without whom she could not live, the one who turned her dreams into reality. With tears of joy in her eyes, she too got down on her knees and hugged him tightly and started to kiss his face, his eyes, and his nose profusely.

"I love you. I love you. I love you, too. I always have Paras. Thank you for everything," she melted in his arms. It was a magical moment for them, they both rekindled their love and passion like never before. "There is still some surprise left, I have booked us a room here to relax and spend some quality time together. Just the two of us." Zunaisa was thrilled to find out that there was more to the whole day and so, she looked forward to it.

After some time, their ride ended and then they checked in their room. When she unlocked the door, the first thing she noticed was, the whole floor was covered with rose petals and the room was dimly lit and decorated with more flowers and candles, she was left awestruck. Paras had brilliantly organised the whole surprise, she was left captivated. They both then made their way to the room and made themselves comfortable on the bed.

They spent the day eating, watching movies together, Paras would occasionally get into a pillow fight with her or would gently wrestle her to the ground. The room was filled with their laughter and joy.

As they were wrestling, Paras had pinned her down while she was still trying to slither away from his tight grip, he suddenly stopped wrestling and pulled her towards him. He deeply gazed into her eyes, as though he was longing for her. Zunaisa brushed his face and hair; she wanted him too, their eyes spoke and craved for each other. He leaned further close and started to run his finger across her hair, face, neck and slowly progressed towards the roundness of her chest and then her navel; she felt a tingling sensation and almost moaned. As they got more and more closer the time seemed to pause, he leaned into her face, their breaths mingled and it felt as though the world had just narrowed down to just the two of them. When his lips finally brushed hers passionately, it was as if everything had fallen into place. The faint scent of his cologne filled her senses while the warmth of her touch drove him crazy; they both wanted each other and knew it was the right moment that they had both waited for so long. This time they didn't want to protest to any doubts neither did either of them want a second away but to surrender and feel each other like never before. They both breathed heavily and as they settled in the moment, the rest of the world and all the right or wrong melted away, leaving just the two of them; relishing the shared moment of intimacy. It wasn't just the closeness of their bodies but the bond had grown stronger and deeper in that unspoken space.

They were wrapped cosily in the blanket together, Zunaisa was peacefully and gently resting on his chest; their hands and fingers entwined as though they were inseparable. He kissed her forehead and hugged her to sleep.

After a while, they woke from their nap; Zunaisa realised that it was close to her curfew time and deadline. They decided to quickly get some supper and leave for home. "I am glad we made it so far. Thank you for everything, babe. I think we both needed this quality time and now that I will be occupied with the wedding and we won't be able to talk or meet as much. This short date is perfect for me to survive the coming few weeks that I would have to be away from you." Paras was happy that his efforts were appreciated, and he knew he needed this time with her too. With her being away for a while for the wedding, it was going to be a tough time for him. But now, at least they had a briefcase full of moments and memories to cherish till they reunite. They both felt fulfilled and content, and finally drove back to their home.

"Come on everyone, we have our flight in the next couple of hours, hurry up. Dad and I are going to the hotel to check on the guests. And my ladies, I will send the car over to you and we shall all meet at the airport," said Rey to the ladies of the house. Everyone was doing their last-minute packing and arrangements, the whole house was in a mess and chaos, but it was a kind of chaos which they were all happy about, after all, it was their dearest Shanaya's wedding, which was going to be the wedding of the year.

The Rizvi family had organised and were hosting a destination wedding to Jaipur and the wedding festivities were to last for a few weeks. All the friends and family met at the airport and boarded their flight for Jaipur. At the resort, the guests were welcomed in a traditional Indian custom with garlands and sorbet; everyone was enthralled and excited with the exemplary hospitality.

There was so much going on and about, managing the guests, the day long events and functions, the evening soiree and much more. The bridesmaids left no stone unturned in organising games and dance performances. Although there were many staff and other bridesmaids and relatives to take care of the things, Zunaisa was toppled with all the hefty responsibilities and being the bride's sister it was her prerogative to ensure and supervise everything went about smoothly. From checking on the guests, to the food menu and other arrangements, ensuring the outfits and fittings for the bride are on time; she was juggling and managing them all.

While she was enjoying the functions and giving her best to everything, she did occasionally miss Paras a lot. With so much going on, she barely got the time to speak to him let alone text him but in her heart, she was at peace, she knew that he wasn't going to go anywhere and the first thing she would do after the wedding was to rush in his arms. Zunaisa had invited Paras to the wedding, she had thought that it could be an icebreaker for him and her family to finally meet him. However, he couldn't join her citing professional commitments and since she was in the same profession; she did understand the gravity of it and did not push him to join them.

In intervening moments, whenever she could find some spare time; she would sneak to either text him or update him with photos and sometimes she would quickly manage to speak to him for a few minutes over the call.

The main festivities of the wedding were: *haldi, mehendi and sangeet*; the guests and the family members swayed and danced their hearts out in all the functions. The themes for the wedding were phenomenal and as was the décor; Shanaya looked ethereal in her pre-wedding festivities and a lot of attention to detail was given duly as per the liking of the bride-to-be. Shanaya and her mother got emotional and everyone felt the depth of the bond the duo shared. Weddings although are full of festivities but one cannot take away from it that it is a life altering decision. Rey tried to lighten the mood and said, "Finally, you will be married off. What a relief!" Everyone then burst into laughter and resumed their merry-making.

Just then Zunaisa started to notice that Paras had been continuously calling her which was quite unlikely of

Paras. She politely excused herself to answer the call. And when she answered it, she could hear him sobbing and crying out loud; she got really worried. "Paras? Babe? What happened? Why are you crying? I am sorry, I couldn't take your calls. Hello? Are you there?" For several minutes, all he did was to cry and then finally he told her, "Ever since you left, the situation at home changed for bad, Dad wasn't keeping well at all. And suddenly my dad? He had a heart attack a couple of days ago; he has been in ICU since then. It's been days that you are gone and I don't know what to do, everyone at home is losing it. I can't do this alone. I don't know how to handle it. What if dad doesn't make it? Why are you not here when I need you the most, Zunaisa You are busy with your stupid wedding. Do I not matter to you at all? On top of it, you barely have the time to even speak to me when I need it the most. I guess, Mom and Dad are right about her, and you? You are just so selfish," he couldn't stop crying.

She was taken aback by his strange remarks, he sounded so lost, bitter and different but the gravity of what he told was far more grave than to take offence of what accusations he was hurling at her. She felt helpless, here the love of his love was tearing apart and on the other side, her sister was getting married. She didn't know what to do; how could she be available at both the places? She tried to calm him down and console him, "Babe! I am here with you. Please don't cry. I love you. I will come to you as soon as I can. I promise. But right now, I really can't leave the wedding in between but I promise I will come soon. Uncle, would be fine soon. Please hold yourself, babe." But Paras didn't really care to listen to her and hung up the call.

Her heart sank and she didn't know what to do, she was put in such a challenging spot; if it was some other family commitment, she would have made an excuse but this was her sister's wedding who stood for her all her life; how could she bail out on her, and on the other hand it was the love of her life. She loathed at her doleful plight and thought to herself that as soon as the main festivities and wedding gets over, she will take the first flight to Delhi; even though others had planned to stay back at the resort for a while but she made up her mind that she would waste no time and meet Paras right away.

THE WALK OF THORNS

Finally, the big day arrived, and everyone gathered around their dearest Shanaya, offering their wishes, love and luck for the new chapter of her life that was about to begin. Everyone was emotional and happy; tears of sorrow and joy were rolling down in torrents all around. Shanaya hugged her parents and siblings, even though they had promised that they wouldn't cry but, in that moment, everybody was overwhelmed and naturally so, tears of joy rolled down their cheeks. It was a tough time for the family but seeing Shanaya happy and content is all they ever wanted, thereby, with wet eyes and big smiles they bid her farewell.

After the wedding got over and all the guests and family retreated to their rooms to rest. This was the right time for Zunaisa to excuse herself from the post celebration and work on her exit to go and meet Paras. She quickly took a brief opportunity to explain the whole situation to her friends, they all decided to help her plan a strategy to meet Paras, convince her parents, and make the necessary arrangements for her travel.

"Here, I have booked your flight. You just go and tell Uncle and Aunty that an urgent matter has come up and we will stay back here to back you up in any case," Monica added. Zunaisa was overwhelmed by the support, she could no longer wait to go and see Paras. "I'll just contact Anirudh on Instagram and get his address, and I know he will be on board with the plan," said Zunaisa. She contacted Anirudh on Instagram and to her surprise he immediately responded, she explained her idea of surprise visit to Paras and Anirudh was more than happy to know. "This is an awesome idea; I will send you the address. And since you will be here in a couple of hours; it would be perfect if you surprise him at his house. He is home alone. Everyone is at the hospital; they would likely spend the whole night there. So, this is your perfect chance. He really has missed you a lot while you were away. And don't worry, I won't spoil the surprise or tell him a word; you just come here and cheer my man up," said Anirudh.

She was overjoyed to have his support, her heart ached to be reunited with him. Thereafter, she quickly ran to her parents and told them that she urgently needed to go back to Delhi because her office needed her for some important work. She promised them to sort things out and be back soon. Her parents knew that their daughter was very ambitious and passionate about her career and after dutifully discharging all her familial obligations it was only fair for them to let her go and attend to her other important errands; and without a fuss they agreed and allowed her to go. She was happy but at the same time, she had a sense of guilt choking her for lying to her parents. All through her life she never lied or tried to conceal anything from her parents but at that moment she couldn't really afford to tell them what all was happening in her life. She hugged them and quickly hailed a cab for the airport.

"H/61, looks like this is it. This is his house. Hmm, I cannot wait to go and hug him tightly. I promise babe this was the last time that you ever had to be alone without me," she said to herself. She was nervous and excited; she walked to the main door which was already unlatched. The main door promptly led to a tiny passage which finally connected his hallway, strangely enough the hallway gate was also carelessly left open. She was a little confused seeing how the whole house was left unlocked and unattended but she thought maybe Paras was too consumed and lost to care. She walked a few steps in and nearly collapsed on the floor at what she saw; her eyes refused to believe what they had just witnessed; she was astonished and shocked beyond limits.

To her it felt as if her worst nightmare had come true, she saw the love of her life with none other than Priya. They were so lost in their moment of passion and kissing each other to even notice that Zunaisa stood there watching them while her heart sank, and she felt as though someone had stabbed her heart.

She screamed, "Paras!" They both got shocked and quickly got up. Paras couldn't believe that Zunaisa was here and caught him in such a compromising position. He didn't know what to say and what to do, Priya tried to intervene and tell Zunaisa but Paras stopped her. "Zunaisa, I can explain. This is not what it looks like. You are mistaken. Priya was just here to support, she has been looking after everyone at home almost every day and it is just nothing, okay?" Zunaisa couldn't believe how disgusting Paras was being at the moment, she clearly saw him kissing another woman and not just any woman; this was the girl who had created so much nuisance in their lives. She went all the way without eating or sleeping just to reunite with him and surprise him, but instead, he left her in a surprise and how. It was such a horrific surprise that it was going to haunt her for the rest of her life. "Are you kidding me, Paras? I caught you with this girl red-handed and you are still mansplaining me? You make me sick; I left everything back and came here to surprise you. I thought you needed it but here you are seeking comfort and pleasure with her. Paras, what did I ever do to deserve this?" She shattered and couldn't stop crying, it felt to her as if hell had broken loose on her.

Priya intervened, "Well, Paras might not tell you off. But I will. I am not just anybody, I have been his support for as long as I have been alive and I plan to do that till the day I die. You were too busy to care and were having your gala time at the wedding, dancing and goofing around. And here, my Paras and his family? They were in so much pain and agony but you were clearly too lost in your whole world to care. And now, you are here out of nowhere and you think you are doing him a favour? Just get a life, Zunaisa." To her utter dismay, Paras didn't even try to stop Priya from brewing such conspiracy and hurling such mean words at her; in fact, she could recall that Paras told her the exact same words over the phone call. Everything now started to add up, she was able to piece everything bit by bit, realising as to what had ensued. Paras was vicariously speaking Priya's words; she knew that she had lost him now. his complete silence on the entire conversation needed no more explanation. However, she still urged him to give her an explanation.

"What more explanation do you want Zunaisa, please stop with this hue and cry; you are only embarrassing yourself here. Priya is right, I kept calling you, I needed you but you were too busy in your world to care. You knew I had problems at home, my family isn't ideal like yours, I told you. I took you as my own and I would keep telling you to be there for me but you are just so selfish. Now, I am done with you and your so-called love. I want to be with someone who will be there for me when I need them and not with someone like you who only decides to come when it is convenient for her." His words pierced her heart like swords and she felt her skin being shred to pieces. The man to whom she gave her all, within a moment brushed her off and severed all ties. She couldn't believe what she was hearing.

She ran to him and fell on his feet, she begged him, "Paras, please don't do this to me. I have loved you with all my heart, I did whatever I could. I chose you over my family all the time. Please, don't leave me like this babe, I...I...I couldn't leave the wedding in between but look I came here, I am with you. I will just forget all this ever happened and I promise I will never question you but please don't leave me. I love you, I can't live without you, Paras...please," she whimpered and cried uncontrollably. But Paras didn't turn a deaf ear to her, it seemed that all the love and affection he had was gone.

He knocked her off his leg so fiercely that she crashed to a nearby glass table and ended up being hurt. And he didn't even bother to check on her if she was grievously hurt, she was humiliated and heartbroken. "You are only creating a mess. Let me tell you once and for all, I am breaking up with you. We anyway didn't have any relationship in the first place neither did I ever think if we could ever be married. My family wants me to marry Priya and I think their choice is right. I need to be with someone who will care for me selflessly and be with me at all times and you Zunaisa? You are not the one for me. Now don't force me to drag you out and just leave." After such humiliating and insulting words, she knew there was no point for her to stay back or even ask him for any explanation. His words and his intentions were pretty clear.

She got up and gathered herself, her tears were uncontrollable. She left his house and started to aimlessly walk on the road, every passerby and cars would look at her stunned and dumbfounded. A well-dressed girl who seemed to belong to a good family, walking aimlessly on the road. She also got a cut on her forehead, when she crashed at the table but that physical pain was nothing compared to the pain she was feeling from within. A couple times she almost walked on the main road and missed by a few seconds from meeting with an accident.

One middle aged man angrily got down from the car and went to her, "Have you lost your mind? Who walks like this in front of a busy road like that? What if you met with an accident? What will your parents feel? These kids today are so incorrigible." He noticed she was zoned out and didn't say a word back, all she was doing was to cry. He saw the injury on her forehead, he got alarmed; he knew that something was wrong. He seemed like a fairly good man; he sat her down on the pavement and offered her some water. "My dear, are you okay? Where is your family? Come, let me help you book a cab for your home. Your family must be worried for you." The gentleman helped her to book a cab home, he sat her down in the car hoping that she safely reached her home.

She reached her home and settled the cab bill and walked in. The whole house was empty and quiet, the only noise she could hear was her sighing and crying; her whole world had come crashing down. She didn't know what to do, who to call, what happened, and why it happened the way it did. "This can't be true. Why would he do this? I thought of a lifetime with him and he just dumped me like that? What is my fault? Was it that I loved him? Is that my mistake?" She kept on weeping and howling so loudly that her voices echoed throughout the entire house. She knew this was not a sudden decision from his end, how could it be, she knew that Priya was always there in the picture and even though her gut instincts told her to back off but she barely paid attention to it. She was highly self-critical and started to bash herself for everything, even though his actions were unjustified and uncalled for, she blamed herself for it.

She whispered to herself, "Everyone, everyone told me that he was not the right guy. That I was going wrong and I was losing myself and now look? As much as I wanted to prove all of them wrong but they were proved right instead. How will I face them? My friends, my family. I left them all for him, I came here for him and he just didn't care. Why do I always have to suffer? Am I not worthy of being loved? Am I not sufficient?" She had so many doubts, questions, unattended feelings running through her mind, she was in such a chaos. She lay on the floor, crying for hours and hours.

After sometime, she noticed her phone had been ringing for a while now; she still thought that it was Paras, so she hurriedly got up to answer it. But to her disappointment it wasn't him, it was Annie, with a shivering hand and quivering voice she answered her call. "Zee? What happened? Why are you crying? Is everything okay? Uncle and Aunty wanted me to check on you. What's wrong?" Zunaisa broke down completely on the call and reiterated the entire episode to her. Annie couldn't believe what she was hearing. She was shocked and disgusted but she knew she had to calm Zunaisa down first before getting into the nuances. "Look, you are not alone. Get it? Monica, I and Apala will take the next flight to Delhi and we are coming to you. But please, Zee, hold yourself and don't do anything crazy okay? I will handle things with Uncle and Aunty. Just stay put. Okay love?" Zunaisa did not have the bandwidth to even answer fully, she only spoke with fillers and hung up the call.

That night was the worst night of her life, every second of it weighed on her. Seconds felt like hours and years, she was writhing and loathing in pain. She had such a sharp shooting ache in her heart as though she was having a heart attack, but that is what a heartbreak does to you. It breaks you apart, the wounds are not visible to the naked eyes but the scars and pain it leaves you with are so no inexplicably excruciating that no medicine in the world can remedy it. The pain of a heartbreak has to be borne by the heartbroken. She had everyone in her life except the one she considered her entire life was now gone and she was left all to deal with this pain and anguish all alone.

She thought to herself: all of this while her only true and loyal partner has been her grief and sorrow; we all can celebrate the moments of joy and fun with everyone. But the pain? It is such a loyal emotion that unlike any other it has to be dealt on its own, bore on its own and we have to come out of it on our own.

Some people do get lucky like Zunaisa to have supporting friends and family but even they cannot fully comprehend the intensity and agony she might be going through. She spent the night crying; at some intervals she would have the urge to call him but she stopped herself. She wept endlessly till sleep overtook her. Early in the morning her doorbell rang, Zunaisa's friends were there; she attended the door. They all ran to embrace her, she looked so different, tired and exhausted. Her eyes were swollen, her lips were parched, her hair flying carelessly, she collapsed in Monica's arms. They couldn't bear the sight of her, she was in such a miserable state, they saw the injury on her forehead and felt sickened and nauseous. They couldn't believe it was the same lively and chirpy Zunaisa, it felt that her heart and happiness had been ripped apart. When she saw them, she couldn't help and wept more and more. They tried their best to console her but sadly nothing of it worked much.

"I am going to teach this man a lesson, how dare he do this with you? He cheats on you and blames you instead? Does he know anything about relationships? I warned you, Zee. I told you that he has disrespected you once and this man will do it again. But you didn't listen," Apala said. Monica pitched in, "Ugh, come on there is no point in discussing why it happened and what Zee did. It is pretty much clear that this guy wanted the best of both worlds and he knew was ultimately going to marry this Priya girl. He just found a good enough reason to break ties with her. God, I feel sick. Now, let us just forget all of this and try to freshen her up and go out. She can't be here crying day and night. Listen to me Zee, life doesn't end if a person leaves. Have faith in God, whatever happens, happens for a reason. You deserve better and your tears are way too precious to be wasted on him. You have already cried enough, let's get you dressed. We will go around the city a bit and watch a nice movie together, okay?" They all agreed and thought it was a good idea, thinking it might help Zunaisa declutter her thoughts and she would have a fresh breath of air.

They took her out for a drive, thereafter for some food and movie; but nothing seemed to interest her. She was so consumed by her remorse that nothing truly mattered to her, she kept on recalling the whole episode and sometimes she would have the flashback of their good times together, from the first meeting, to the beautiful drives and countless dates.

When we try to move on from something or someone or cope up with a loss, our mind often tries to replay the good moments making the whole healing process even more difficult than it is.

They knew she was going to take her time to cope up and move on, therefore, they decided to let her be and work through the grief at her pace. But till her family returns they all decided to stay back with her for a few more days; so that she wouldn't feel left all alone.

At some nights, she would strangely wake up and have panic attacks and on the other days she barely ate food. Although, her friends tried to comfort her, nothing seemed to be working. She knew and appreciated that her friends were trying so much but it was as if her heart was torn in a manner that moving on and coping with it became next to impossible for her.

THE JADED LOVER

Days were passing by and Zunaisa's health was deteriorating. She had stopped eating, going out, she would curl up herself in bed all day and sleep the whole time. Monica, Annie and Apala could no longer see her like that, they thought that only her parents could offer her the true warmth and comfort she needed. Even though they had promised her that they wouldn't tell her parents about whatever had happened but seeing her in such pain and drastic condition, they unanimously decided to inform her parents and Rey about the whole situation.

When they broke the news to them, they all were shocked, angry and extremely hurt. Rey in fact, got so violent at the news that he couldn't wait to go and teach the guy a lesson but his parents calmed him down. Nikhat broke down at the news, "Oh my poor child! I was feeling so uneasy and now I know why. My child is in so much pain. This is what I was scared about. I had a feeling she might get hurt. It's my fault. Aquib, please book the tickets as soon as possible. I want to go to my child," she cried to him. Aquib wasted no time and booked their flight for Delhi.

Soon, they all reached home and when they saw Zunaisa; their eyes were stunned in utter shock and their heart sank. Nikhat ran to her and hugged and kissed her. Zunaisa looked very weak, her under eyes had become hollow and almost brown, they all had never seen Zunaisa like this ever before.

They wished they could take her pain away but sadly they couldn't. Nikhat knew she needed time to recuperate, therefore they all decided to give her some space and not force her for anything. After a few days, her friends also left since they all had to resume their work, but they insisted and pleaded Zunaisa to stay in touch. After the incident, she had stopped going to the office and had resigned as well; she didn't have the gumption to face Paras ever again.

The day she left her resignation email, she noticed a few calls from Paras; she was tempted to answer them but she was reminded of the insult, the betrayal; she decided not to take those calls. She knew she had brushed off her instincts in the past and it led to such a mess; she wasn't ready to be bitten twice. He kept calling her at different intervals and days; on one such day, he left her a message, *"I am standing outside your house. I want to talk to you once. Please come down."* It made no sense to her, after all this while what did he want from her? She thought to herself, "What do you want from me now? You stole what was left of my heart and now I have lost you forever. You ripped me and my heart apart and I am barely able to sew it back; but now I have decided, even with these ripped seams, I shall tie myself together, I promise to myself, never to be ripped off like this again, never to be tore apart again." She ignored his message while the tears streamed down her eyes without restraint.

She had locked herself for days in her room and the girl who once loved admiring and pampering herself; had now lost the will to even look at herself in the mirror or even live. She felt abandoned and lost, she was reminded of her love with Aditya; she couldn't help but relate how a man yet again even after she moved heaven and earth; left her high and dry while she writhed in agony, questioning her very being. She was slowly getting convinced that maybe love is not meant for her even though she craved it all her life, but now she was too mortified to be vulnerable again, to fall in love again, to open up to someone again. From being a part of his love story to now being just a longing story; a lot changed. She did all she could and put in as much of an effort that she could but nothing was going to overshadow his lack of effort, thereof.

She was broken yet again and had another failed attempt at love. She felt estranged, forsaken, deserted; she lost a soul which she dearly endeared and was left cold and heartbroken. She did not know what to do, she kept on questioning her choices, her destiny. Where was she supposed to be? And why was it so hard for her to wish ill for people, even if they were the ones who wronged her? At times she wished to be like someone who would never care about emotions or love, but how could she stop being who she was?

She was a person who wanted to give love and to be loved; not that she expected a lot because she knew had a heart filled with love, oceans of love and she knew wasn't just an ordinary lover, she was a courageous and bold lover, who could go to any lengths. She knew the kind of love she could give. She wasn't expecting anybody to love her with the same intensity but only wished and hoped for someone to at least come half a mile with her. She wanted to be loved for who she was, how she was and not solely be desired for looks, her body or other superficial things. She knew that there was more to a person than just looks, for her the idea of beauty was skin deep, she found inner beauty more meaningful. She knew that most of us were drawn to anything which seemed appeasing to our bewildering eyes; we are drawn to it just like moths are drawn to a flame. And often, it is so, that what may please our eyes may not please our soul.

She really did try her level best to make Paras the happiest man and in the due course she even lost her own identity, her true self, but she was so hopelessly in love to understand that she was digging her own grave. She kept giving him chances again and again and again even though she deeply knew down within that he was slowly messing with her head, mind and heart piece by piece. Yet, she was tied to her hopes and believed that one fine day, he may change for good; and would love her with all his heart and give her all his loyalty. But how can you change someone if they aren't the right fit for you in the first place?

The things that are not meant for you or don't align with you will never bring you peace no matter how much your heart wants or craves it. Therefore, the only wise thing is to swallow the bitter pill now so that you don't have to suffer and succumb to the pain later; the sooner you rip off the band-aid, the quicker your healing journey begins.

As much as we want to take control of our lives, we just cannot do that; you may plan all the plausible strategies and have blueprints but if God hasn't destined it for you, all your relentless pursuits to achieve your goal will stand futile at face of the divine decree.

We also need to understand that we cannot control people or their behaviour but we can definitely change what is within our prowess; and that is: our actions and reactions. The change comes and begins from us and we should hold the power to walk away with our head held high in spirits with the firm faith that what we truly deserve will come to us even if it is poles apart and miles away from us, God will bring and facilitate it for us.

She was lying on her bed lifelessly when she heard her phone ring frantically but she didn't really have the energy to take the call but when the call continued; she picked it up and answered. "What is it, Apala? You know, I am not in a mood to talk. I will call you later." But before Zunaisa could hang up the call Apala quickly retorted, "Listen to me Zunaisa, you won't believe what I saw on Priya's profile. These guys got hitched last night. Let me send you the photos." Zunaisa's phone slipped from her hand, she stood in shock, unable to believe what she had just heard. "Are you? Are you sure? How could this be? He was calling me for the past couple of days and now this? Apala, I…I…" She crumbled and collapsed into sobs. She drew the courage from the bottom pit of her stomach and checked the photos Apala had sent. She saw them together; this was for real. Paras and Priya were hitched and engaged; her heart sank.

"I don't even know how to react anymore, I want to cry till I possibly become unconscious or just came out of this like a bad dream but all my love, all tears have been used up. I am empty. I have nothing left in me. I never ever in my life abandoned anybody, he was the love of my life but how can I hold back someone who had already decided to leave?"

Apala tried to console her but she knew the pain she was going through was too intense and no matter how much she wanted to help or pacify her; her words couldn't suffice it.

When the march of time erodes and the throes of love unfold, people drop their masks and reveal their true selves. But by then, it is often too late for us to come back or run away from them. We often end up giving the wrong people the best version of ourselves. To her Paras was now nothing but a forgotten fantasy which had to let go off. At the end they both had somehow failed in this relationship; he did not know how to love her and she could not have him.

She sat alone in her room consumed by her feelings of inadequacy but then in those deep shallow moments of darkness, a voice from within echoed which no longer wanted to be a part of this painful journey anymore.

You do not necessarily need a closure to close the doors and chapters or to burn the bridges; sometimes the inaction should be enough of a catalyst for you to take action and move on from what no longer serves a purpose in your life. You may not be fully able to move on within a day or few weeks but everything that doesn't kill you only makes you stronger. You just need to resist the urge to become a prisoner of your own thoughts. The moment you understand that every setback is a setup for you to bounce back up for something greater, you will then start to wear your challenges and scars with immense pride. Not everything you lose is a loss. It is all about perspective.

No person has it all figured out, we often fail to show kindness and consideration to ourselves when push comes to shove. We try to be extremely patient and loving, if someone close to us is suffering then why do we slack off in treating ourselves with the same love and affection we generously give to others? The only voice that truly matters is yours, the way you think about yourself, the way you talk to yourself. When we are left to the lurch, don't we wipe our own tears? Don't we pull ourselves when our heart sinks? Don't we push ourselves for that one more rep in the gym? Don't we fight the storms and survive the downfall all by ourselves?

Then why can't we applaud ourselves, our body, our mind and be gentle with our hearts? For the first time in a while she spoke to herself with no judgement. She slowly began to realise that it wasn't her fault after all. Those photos were enough of a reason for her to stop brooding and loathing in her loss. She finally decided to channelise her energy to a better use. She realised that sometimes a loss is the ultimate gain. Perhaps that job you lost wasn't right for you, that lover who cheated on you perhaps wasn't meant for you, that friend you lost perhaps was an enemy in disguise; often our human minds likely associate loss as a setback but sometimes that loss may actually be the ultimate gain.

We humans are definitely one of the most complex creatures and are perpetually flawed. We may know what is right and what is fatal for us, yet we all become weak and surrender to our innate desires. We all have addictions and choose our own poison without which we feel a void: a void that could only be quenched with that poison we deliriously desire, even if it comes at the cost of being fatal to our every atom of being, we still would blithely crave and pursue it.

But does it mean that we cannot break this vicious cycle? We most certainly can, the change begins from within. And with all these contemplation and moments of reflection; Zunaisa was now ready to take charge of her life again.

A few days later, everyone was surprised to see Zunaisa sitting at the breakfast table. She greeted everyone and sat with the family to spend some time with them. She realised that in a way her behaviour was equally impacting her family. While she wouldn't eat or drink, the whole house would also stay gloomy but after a long time, the house was filled with waves of happiness to see her trying to take tiny steps to be better. She had missed this for a while now, the following day she spent all day with the family and planned to visit her favourite park. Everyone happily agreed, even though she had not fully recovered, she knew she deserved another shot in life, she just couldn't give up like that.

For the first time in a while, she got up and did her old routine of getting ready and being nicely dressed. While she was browsing her wardrobe contemplating what she should wear, her eyes got locked on the red dress; it was the same red dress she was wearing when she first met Paras, the dress evoked a lot of memories. She had cherished it for the longest of time but now that the reason behind it was only a faint and distant memory; she decided to wear that same red dress as a symbol to orchestrate her liberation and bolster her confidence from within. She had to let go of the memories and move on.

She put on her red dress and paired it with her darkest shade of red lipstick; she realised that she had missed being herself. But now she was determined to regain and come out of it much stronger, confident and as a better person.

They reached the park, to her it felt as though she had stepped out after ages. She missed the fresh clean air, the greenery, the nature, she couldn't help but notice the bustling surrounding and startling faces. She could hear the birds chirping, the kids running around and playing, at some distance she saw some families feasting and enjoying their picnic. She smiled at the sight and then she took off her heels and stood barefoot on the ground, trying to soak in nature and the surroundings; she felt rejuvenated. There was so much in life to be thankful about and so much beauty around the world to see; everything contained beauty, but it is just that not everyone sees it. The family spent the evening together, chatting and enjoying like good old times, although they did miss Shanaya, but they were content with the fact that she was happily married now.

Zunaisa was now slowly recovering, the entire incident had taken a toll on her mentally and physically. She had lost a lot of weight and often had frequent panic attacks coupled with severe fits of anxiety. She decided to seek professional help and therapy to regain her life and confidence. She was gradually taking steps to become better and her family supported her through and through.

Aquib sat with Zunaisa; he knew every detail of what had happened so far with her beloved daughter but he just couldn't gather himself to talk it through with her. Seeing their child fight for their life and seeing them experience a tormenting heartbreak is one of the worst of nightmares for any parent. Although Nikhat would regularly talk and share things with her, Aquib didn't have the courage to speak to her freely about whatever had happened. Fathers and brothers have their own way of expressing their feelings and emotions, they may or may not be outspoken or provide unequivocal verbal support, but they always stand by you like solid pillars.

But that day, he finally spoke to her, "I see you are getting better now. I hope the therapy sessions are doing you good. Why don't you apply for an internship and get back to work? After all, I have yet to come across someone who is as passionate about law as you are,

Zunaisa. You are a brave girl and I am proud of you. And you deserve the best man alive who will love you more than all of us collectively can." Aquib's eyes became numb, he continued, "My love, I am going to tell you something and I want you to remember and retain this for life even after I am long gone. Dear, have you ever looked at the Sun? You see how it still shines bright even though sometimes it is behind the clouds? Similarly, if you are facing difficulties in life right now, nothing still has the power to dull your brightness. You are as powerful and as bright as the Sun, you just need to believe in yourself; that no matter what the situation is, you'll always shine on, honey. Just don't you ever give up. We all are here for you." Tears rolled down her cheeks when she heard her father speak his heart out to her, she hugged and thanked him for his unconditional love and support.

She reminded herself that there was more to her life than Paras, she had so many dreams and aspirations that she wanted to achieve. She decided to pay heed to her father's advice and started to apply for new internships. She wasn't going to give up on her dream of becoming a lawyer because of a setback. Although Shanaya wasn't around, she would check up on her each day and her mother offered her continuous warmth and support. On some days she would tag her for evening walks, on other days she would spend time massaging her hair or watching stand-up comedies and other many other things that Zunaisa liked.

Zunaisa thanked God, for such a loving and understanding family; who became her support and lifeline through it all. They all were trying to mend a heart which they hadn't even broken.

THE BRAVE HEART

...You could be a wonderful parent at 18, a business tycoon at 50 or simply a content homebody at 70, and irresistible for the rest of your life. We are constantly ambushed by the preordained societal norms which we as individuals feel compelled to adhere to. But there are billions of people and billions of stars and they all carry a light, heavenly vivid and unique to their own. You are not too late, you are not too lost, you are planted where you are exactly meant to be. Your journey is unique to you, and you shall bloom in your own time, at your own pace. Yes, you will have many different and difficult challenges, but they will only shape you further and make you unique amongst the billions. Just trust yourself and the process...

She desperately wanted to get back on her feet, she started to incorporate prayers and meditation in her morning routine; she found her peace in it. While she was starting to take care of her mental health, it was tantamount to monitor her physical health as well which had tremendously suffered. She noticed that her face had lost the shine and spark; she wanted to fix it, so, therefore, she started to observe healthy and balanced meals that would nourish her body and skin. She gradually started to make progress with it.

In one of the sessions her therapist encouraged her to join a gym or to indulge in some new hobbies or activities.

She went to her parents and told them that she wanted to join the gym and without any second thought, her parents agreed, they wanted to support her journey to recovery and healing in whatever capacity they could. Although, now that she had the permission from her family, a heads up from her therapist, she still had traces of doubts and sadness which would occasionally creep in and suck out her energy to an extent that it would end up messing with her normal day to day life. Therefore, in order to tackle the monotony and not let her impending sadness suck away her energy, she decided to make her gym routine interesting.

She decided to treat herself and went shopping to get herself some new activewear for her workouts. After a long time, she was feeling like her old self, who used to enjoy going out, doing things, and taking care of herself. To her that entire experience felt liberating, she tried on lots of clothes and shopped till she dropped, thereafter, she treated herself with her favourite coffee and got herself some jewellery and few other stuffs that she liked.

Life had started to pick up its pace slowly. She gradually began to shift and lead a routine life. That one solo date led to many more solo dates; she slowly began to be on her own and truly started to enjoy her solitude. She revived her old hobbies of writing and would often go out to her favourite coffee shops and parks to enjoy her time. It was one of her desires and on her bucket list to learn swimming and horse riding. So, she enrolled herself for these classes and would spend her weekends there. Her life was truly getting transformed for the better, and she slowly started to embrace the change, and gradually began to enjoy every bit of it.

One fine day, she was trying to look for some photos in her gallery and somehow while scrolling up and above; she happened to see the album in her phone which had all of the photographs of Paras and her. She tried hard to resist the urge to not open it but she failed and started to flick through all the photos, reminiscing about them. Her teardrops fell on one of the photos, she relapsed and was reminded of all the love and those intricate shared moments they had together. She had never shared such a bond with anyone except Paras, her heart softened at the thought of him; questions began to loom in her mind.

She opened the last message that he had sent her which said that he wanted to meet her and weeks later he got engaged to Priya. She thought to herself, "What if he wanted to confess his feelings and tell me that he was going to get engaged, or what if he was calling me to get back to him? How will I never know? Did I impulsively take a leap of faith and moved on? We shared such a nice time together, all of it cannot be fake, I should call him." Her chest tightened, and tears started cascading in waves. When she was about to dial him, just then Rey entered the room. "Zee! Zee, what happened? Why are you crying and why on earth are you calling this man? Give me your phone. You have to delete his number and his entire existence, Zee. What are you even thinking? This man threw you under the bus, you have suffered enough. You cannot go back to him. Please just let it go." He hugged and tried to console her, but she broke down in his arms seeking comfort. He continued, "As a man I am telling you, we know, we just know, the moment we see a girl, we know that she is the one that we want to spend our lives with. We can go to any lengths for her but what he did to you, that's not something a man in love does. You might think it was your fault or that girl came out of nowhere but I am telling you she was always there. That man never ever explicitly proposed to you for marriage and goes ahead to marry this girl out of nowhere? It was clearly a conscious decision he made. Do you know a man in love will never shy away from a serious commitment and will commit to the one he truly loves. It was all frivolous from his side. You cannot go back to him or even second guess if he had anything to say to you at all, if only you did, you would find more lies and manipulation. He just enjoyed and thrived on your energy and support. And trust me you deserve better than this. Just let him go, Zee. He no longer serves a purpose in your life. Just take the lesson and move on. Forget about him, please."

She realised in that moment of weakness she was about to make another blunder, had Rey not entered and stopped her; she would have really made a grave mistake. She knew that Rey made sense and she promised him that she would leave him and eliminate him for good. That night she gathered and mustered every ounce of courage that she had in her and sat with her phone and started to delete all the photos, messages, call logs that she had of him, one by one; it was her attempt at erasing and wiping him away from her memory and life. Although each photo and messages and the story behind it vividly ran through her mind. She suddenly had a realisation that there wasn't anything greatly special in him. In fact, it was her love, her emotions, the unfathomable outpour of feelings that she showered at him; that made him special.

She realised if she could love someone so wrong so passionately then why can't she love herself and direct all her efforts for herself. After all, she stood and survived such a wavy ride, there was a time she had lost the will to live and in her moments of darkness she had attempted a couple of times to end her life as well; but now the kind of realisation she had, it rekindled her passion to live her life to the fullest. It struck her that the love she had endlessly sought in others and in Paras had always been quietly residing within her all along and she just wasn't able to see that until that very realisation kicked in. She promised herself to give her the due love and efforts, she had selflessly been giving to the wrong people.

It wasn't that she was going to stop being who she was but she also realised that you are born alone, and you shall die alone and the longest relationship you will ever have would be the one you have with yourself. So, you must first fall in love with yourself, be comfortable and grounded in your being and then the right person will come to you. Afterall, if you don't love yourself? Who will?

She gave herself the closure and decided to end the chapter with him, that no longer served any purpose in her life; she began to delete all the photos, all the moments, all the memories, permanently. This act of hers demonstrated her resilience and how she was ready to begin a new chapter of her life.

Miracles are not necessarily to be found and sought for in the norms of extraordinary, in fact it could also be seen in everyday moments of life like the sun that rises from the east, the moon shinning bright on a dark night, the sky beautified with constellations and ultimately the true miracle lies in you: you are the unsung hero of your life. You deserve a pat on the back for how far you have come.

As the new journey began, she started to pay more attention to herself, took frequent salon visits; she got herself spa, manicures, pedicures and everything she could to feel and look better. She also started to enjoy and developed a newfound interest in workouts; and it slowly began to be an integral part of her life and self-care regime. The adrenaline rush post workout filled her senses and uplifted her spirits in a way that she felt a high that couldn't be articulated in words. Every day she would look up to go to the gym and try something new to challenge herself and her strength.

On many of her visits to the gym, she noticed that there was this guy who would always be around whenever she was there. At several instances she felt that he may be looking or eyeing at her. It was difficult not to notice him, he was a man who drew eyes effortlessly, everyone would quickly steal a moment to look at him; to say that he was gorgeous may be an understatement.

Every inch of him screamed style and every stride he took projected confidence and his strong presence was truly felt. He had an athletic build which clearly hinted that he spent hours pushing his limits at gym, he looked like on any given day he could deadlift and bench-press without breaking a sweat. He stood tall and towering close to six feet; there was something primal in his energy which screamed rawness and manliness. Surprisingly, Zunaisa was keenly observant of how this man looked and behaved, her instincts and hunch indicated her that there was something about him. She noticed that even though the whole gym couldn't stop gushing over him; his eyes were always pretty much fixated on her. He would ensure that their workout timings would match and would quietly look after her from a distance.

Zunaisa was undoubtedly the most attractive lady there but what drew him closer and keener was that she wasn't ever seen obsessing or gloating over his looks. She would mind her own business, workout and leave without paying much attention to the surroundings or people. The first time that he saw her, she was wearing a sleek, fitted deep plum activewear that hugged her figure in all the right places and hinted at the strength beneath the surface. She was already perfect the way she was but the zest with which he saw her working out suggested that she wished to sculpt, refine and sharpen herself. He noticed a faint sheen of sweat on her which gorgeously glistened on her skin and added more allure and glow to her. She was herself, natural, with no filters or intention to impress anyone but herself and since then, he just couldn't stop but be naturally drawn to her, but he was a respectful man and knew that she wasn't a girl who would accept callous advances.

Days passed but he often failed to muster the courage to go speak to her but whenever she would need help lifting weights or dumbbells, she found him prompt and ready to extend help. The max Zunaisa would do was to give him a smile in return and then resume her workout; he was an attractive man and there were no lee ways about it, however, she didn't have the heart to trust someone again yet.

It was one of those days where she was working out in the gym and was trying to get her posture correct for a squat but time and again, she was failing. When she was about to give up and was heading for some other exercise, a man gently patted her on the shoulder and a deep husky voice followed, "You almost got the stance correct, why are you quitting now? You look like a fierce fighter. Come on, let me help you with your posture." Zunaisa was surprised but she sportingly took his help. While he voluntarily stayed back, and helped her through the whole set. She appreciated his helpful nature but still wasn't sure if she could fully trust him. The man proposed to help her around the workout, "I have been working out since the age of sixteen, I think and if you allow. I can help you with your forms, I can see you have the strength but you just need to get the form correct."

His promptness and eagerness to help her seemed genuine and Zunaisa felt that if she were to gauge every man as a predator that would be wrong of her, so, therefore, she decided to accept his proposal, and let him help in her workouts. Eventually, over a period of time, the invisible walls between them began to fall. What started with prompt help and polite nods, slowly grew into small and light-hearted conversation between sets.

They slowly built a quiet and unspoken comfort and trust; the gym somehow became their space where they both helped and pushed each other to new limits and encouraged one another to be better than yesterday. She realised that he was a very simple guy and never tried to outstep any boundary and respectfully maintained distance. He took utmost care to ensure she felt comfortable. They soon became gym buddies and started working out together every day. It was in no time that they also became good friends, too, he was a fairly decent man; she would often notice that the only girl he spoke to in the gym was her. Sometimes her guts hinted that there could be a possible feeling meandering but she shunned them off before they could even come out. She had made it clear in her mind that she was in no rush to get involved with anybody yet or anytime soon. It was in between one of those days, she thought she should casually speak about the elephant in the room.

"Isn't it funny that it has been a while and I'd like to say that we have become friends and we still don't even know our names. Anyway, I am Zunaisa," she laughed. "Uhh, yeah, you are right. I am such a doofus, such a gorgeous young lady is my gym pal and I still never thought of asking you out for a cup of coffee let alone your name. Well, I will make it up to you, Zuanisa. And by the way you have a very unique name pretty much as unique as mine. My name is Zhulkar. Nice to meet you." They both shook hands and reintroduced themselves. She was happy to find a new friend but something in her mind told her to keep her distance, although, this guy actually gave her no butterflies or anxiety about anything; in fact, she rather felt at ease around him. She never felt like she had to do something out of the way for him, but he would always come up and help her and extend his support to her without a baggage of expectation or reciprocation.

But she had promised herself to keep things slow and focus on herself; she thought it was only fair that she lets him know that she isn't looking for anything else other than friendship, lest he had any feelings. "Well, Zhulkar, I don't know how you will take this but I have recently gone through a terrible episode of a very horrendous breakup, and I genuinely want to focus on myself and my career. I would appreciate your friendship but if you have anything else in mind, I am afraid we will have to part ways right away because I am not in that headspace. And I apologise, if this may come off as rude but I am just being straightforward, I don't see a point in beating around the bush. You are anyway, a fairly good-looking man and you seem decent as well and I am sure, you shall find someone or may already have someone I don't know. I am sorry but I had to say this."

Zhulkar stood surprised to see how much she had bottled up, "Wow! You really delivered a minute of a monologue. Now, I have taken no offence. In fact, I appreciate your point-blank honesty and also thank you for your generous compliments. My mom says that my wife shall be a very lucky woman and I would like to think that she is right. I am not in a zone to get into a relationship either, Zunaisa. I, myself, had a terrible breakup recently and I think I could use a friend like you. How about we just take things slow, start with friendship and if you and I end up liking each other or falling in love which is highly likely because it's two very attractive people, and I would like to say maybe somehow similar too. We may get along really well, you never know. So, one step at a time? Fist bump to that?" she smiled and gave him a fist bump back. There was definitely some spark but both of them were clearly not ready to open up to each other yet, perhaps in time they might but in the moment they both knew they could count on each other as friends. She liked that they both shared something in common and she could definitely use his friendship but falling in love with him was not something that was on her mind. She was definitely open to building an organic friendship with him which lasts forever but of course, she had no ability to foresee what was about to come and only time would tell that.

But she had learnt her mistakes and walked through the storm, she was now a much evolved person who knew that she had to have boundaries and certain parameters that she should never compromise with, and if once, you are disrespected or you feel that the person, be it your lover or friend or anybody for that matter; doesn't actually value your presence or efforts, you should have the courage to walk away and not let them trample you over.

You should choose yourself and not wait to be chosen first. She also had to learn to judge people on what their actions are, somebody could tell you that they love you and they would do anything for you but not everyone means it and some are only there to take advantage suck away all that you have to offer and feed you bread crumbs. And you would find yourself feeding on those crumbs. When you are hungry for love, your heart tends to eat lies. So, it is important to keep yourself full and self-sufficient so that when you actually meet someone that you would like to spend your life with, then they should become a part of your world and not your whole world. Even though you are in love and you must give your all but it must not come at the cost of your peace and your sanity.

"I love you" is perhaps one of the most used words and yet not everyone who says it means it. The meaning of love is not just professing it in words, the essence of it is felt when you accept that nobody is perfect, however, in their imperfection they should try and give in equal effort with their actions, behaviour and gestures; that is the true essence of love. Both of them should walk the mile together and if only one person is more invested than the other; then sadly enough, such a love would barely last and would eventually just end up being a long

forgotten, deep-rooted lesson. Zunaisa had to learn all of this the hard way.

But she was now finally happy in her newfound confidence and new found love that she had discovered from within. For someone who had invested her time in all the wrong places, she had finally learnt to invest it in the right place and that was: in herself, with a hope of a brighter and fulfilling future ahead; Zunaisa started to live her life to the fullest.

Your time and your thoughts that you give and invest in something or someone is the most valuable investment that you will ever make; therefore, make sure that you invest it wisely. And remember, before anything, fall in love with yourself and your life; the only reflection and perception that should matter to you is what and how you feel about yourself. Do you like who you see yourself as in a mirror? Are you a kind person? Are you compassionate? Do you know how to be there for others and especially for yourself? Would you still choose you, when the whole world turns against you? If yes, then know that you, my friend, are on the right path. Love yourself! Your longest relationship will be the one that you have with yourself. Embrace it! And, know that it all starts with you; the real magic lies within you.

EPILOGUE

She thought about all the days of love and war she had gone through; and everything that she went through made her stronger, resilient, and self-sufficient. She had seen a lot, there were some moments that she was going to cherish for a lifetime, and the others were a lesson to be borne in mind forever and a day. But in the end, she felt complete and at peace with herself; she took out her diary and wrote:

"It has been months since you and I have not spoken to each other and parted our ways, but if we were to ever cross paths again; I would look into your eyes although the usual shyness might take over. But I am determined to let you know that even though we were not destined to be together, I believe God has a plan and a better plan for all of us, regardless of what our small minds might want. His plans are greater than our imagination. When you left, I was in pieces, however with time, I picked myself up from those pieces and I finally found the peace from within and the tranquillity that comes with the solitude. I realized that it wasn't you or your love which had the magic, but the magic was in me, I realized that it is my life

and I need to take charge; and perhaps this may be construed as being self-centric but honestly, I now know that I hold the power. I get to decide who deserves a room in my mind and heart and who should stay and who should be left behind. It was a cycle I needed to break, a lesson that I needed to learn to understand who I truly am, and while I would still give my love to all but this time I would invest carefully and protect my peace first and not give away myself profusely to anyone who may not even deserve a slight bit of my love. You wanted me as your muse because you feared me as a lover. It takes a lot of courage to love and to love deeply; and when that VERY love leaves you with scars. You are left alone to heal those scars, those wounds and yourself. Love is never easy, never was and never will be but I am proud that I am a fearless lover and I am not afraid to fall in love again but before that I want to fall in love with myself. I learnt all of this with a lot of hardships and challenges but that is how God strengthens us and teaches us about life!

We are gifted this life, and nobody but your experiences are your best teachers; they teach you how to sail through this gift of life! I am content now, I have no grudges, I don't want any closure for all I know now is that: I am whole before you."

ACKNOWLEDGMENTS

This book is, without a doubt, a piece of my heart. But it would never have come to life without the love, support, and encouragement of the incredible people who stood by me every step of the way. Every word, every chapter, and every thought within these pages has been inspired, shaped, and strengthened by those around me. For that, I am deeply and eternally grateful.

To my parents—you are the foundation of everything I am and everything I aspire to be. Your unconditional love, belief in my dreams, and steady support have been my rock. You have always allowed me to dream big and better, to chase my goals with confidence, and to find my path with your unshakable belief in me.

When I first shared my vision of writing this book, you both, without hesitation, encouraged me to pursue it wholeheartedly. Mom, your ideas and your willingness to always help me have been invaluable, showcasing the lovable, supportive and creative person that you are. Dad, your logical perspective and thoughtful ideas have guided me through this journey, and your doting nature has been my constant source of strength. Your sacrifices, patience, and enduring love have been the roots of my journey. This book is as much yours as it is mine, and I will forever be grateful for everything you have poured into me.

To my kin—Farkhanda and Reyyan, and my next of kin—Jawad; this book is also for you. You have been my pillars of strength, my safe haven, and my greatest supporters, your belief in me has been a guiding light through every challenge, and your unwavering encouragement has inspired me to push beyond my limits, whether through late-night conversations, quiet reassurances, or simply being there when I needed you the most, you have played a vital role in my journey. The power of family, love and unbreakable bonds is something I am reminded of every single day because of you. This journey would not have been the same without the three of you, and I am endlessly grateful for the love and support you've given me.

To my friends—you have been my greatest sources of joy and motivation. While it is impossible to name everyone individually, please know that each of you has played an irreplaceable role in this journey. Your support, in all its forms, has meant more to me than words can express. A heartfelt thanks to Archita, Sarah, Suha, Hassam, Amar, Apurva, Maaz, Anant, Monika, and Hena—my go-to-people. Whether it was through listening to my endless musings, offering thoughtful advice, or cheering me on through the challenges, your presence has been invaluable. To all my friends not mentioned here, the space may be limited, but each of you has a special place in my heart. I treasure every moment, every conversation, and every gesture of support that has brought me close to this dream.

To my incredible team at BlueRose Publishers—thank you for your dedication, commitment, and hard work. A very special and heartfelt mention goes to my core team, especially Rishabh and Rehan, who I rightfully like to call my knights in shining armour. Your steadfast support, meticulous attention to detail, and ability to handle every intricate requirement with patience and precision made all the difference.

Rishabh, in particular, deserves immense recognition for being my go-to-person throughout this journey. As someone who is extremely detail-oriented, I was often demanding, but his patience, ability to execute my vision to perfection, and willingness to go above and beyond to accommodate every instruction truly stood out. From the minutest details to the most significant decisions, he managed everything with remarkable dedication and focus. He was the anchor that kept this process steady through the layers of work, tight deadlines, and endless tweaks. Together you both were truly a calm in the storm, and I cannot thank you enough for your support and tireless effort in making this dream a reality.

To my talented editors, Shreya and Asra, your dedication and insight brought clarity and precision to my words. And to Sadhana, my impeccable designer, thank you for bringing the vision of the book cover to life with such grace and creativity. Even when I had countless tweaks and suggestions, you worked with patience and passion to create something truly remarkable.

To Shirley, Aman, Simran, Amogh, Sakshi, Navreet, Beena and others who worked both on the frontlines and behind the scenes at BlueRose–your contributions have been indispensable. Each of you has been instrumental in ensuring that every detail was handled with care which I truly applaud. Although I cannot name everyone individually, please know that your efforts have been recognised and cherished. Each of you played a significant role in making this book what it is today, and I am forever grateful.

Lastly, to everyone who has supported, inspired, or believed in me–thank you. Your kindness, whether big or small, has left a lasting impact on my journey.

And to my dearest readers–thank you for allowing this book to become a part of your life. *Heightened Love* is a piece of my heart, and I hope it finds a way to yours.

AUTHOR'S NOTE

Writing this book has been one of the most transformative experiences of my life. As I hold the finished work in my hands, I am reminded of the long journey that brought me here–from dreaming of writing a book since the age of 12 to finally seeing that dream materialize. Along the way, I encountered countless breakthroughs and moments of clarity that shaped not only this book but also my perspective on life.

I have always been deeply fascinated by the intricacies of human relationships–their power to elevate us or break us. This book was my way of making sense of the messy, beautiful reality of being human, with the hope that it resonates with anyone who has ever felt the weight of their emotions. In a world where we are often told to suppress our feelings, I wanted this book to emphasize the importance of embracing them. Feeling your emotions, facing them, and expressing them is not a weakness but a profound strength. It is a testament to our resilience and a reminder that being human means allowing ourselves to experience and express the full range of emotions God has gifted us.

At its core, this book is about the universality of emotions. Regardless of where we come from—our countries, cultures, religions, or backgrounds—the essence of being human remains the same. Every one of us feels joy, sadness, love, fear, and hope in our unique ways. Through the story I have written, I have poured my heart into creating something genuine, something I hope you can connect with. Though this book is fiction, I have tried my best to keep it as real as possible, and I believe it has a universal appeal. My hope is that it resonates with anyone who has ever felt the weight of their emotions and the beauty of their experiences.

There were days when the words flowed effortlessly, and others when I lay awake at night, turning over the stories and plots in my mind to ensure that every page brought something of value to the reader. Crafting this book was challenging yet deeply rewarding. Reflecting on this journey, I realise it was as much about healing myself as it was about sharing these stories with you. In the process, I discovered a version of myself I hadn't known before—one that juggled personal life, professional commitments, and this book.

This was not just a project for me; it was a passion. There were days when I spent entire nights writing, completely immersed in the process. On other days, I would carve out moments during court hours to jot down ideas. Sometimes, I would take myself to my favourite coffee shop, sit with my laptop, and work for hours. It was truly an enriching experience—one I will cherish forever.

To you, the reader: thank you for picking up this book. It was written with the hope that it will resonate with your heart, challenge your mind, or simply provide comfort on a difficult day. My story is just one thread in the vast tapestry of human experiences, and I hope it sparks something meaningful in yours.

Finally, to everyone who has been a part of this journey, thank you for believing in me, supporting me, and helping me bring this book to life, your encouragement and faith made all the difference.

Dreams should keep you on your toes and up all night, and *Heightened Love* has truly been that dream for me. It is a piece of me, a piece of my heart, and my passion—and it is now all set to be yours.

www.ingramcontent.com/pod-product-compliance
Lightning Source LLC
LaVergne TN
LVHW041924070526
838199LV00051BA/2711